FAITH TURNS INTO HOPE, HOPE TURNS INTO MIRACLES

J.M.Manning

Paperback: 978-1-969919-24-4
Hardback: 978-1-969919-71-8
eBook: 978-1-969919-25-1
Library of Congress Control Number: 2025922279

This is a work of fiction.

Ordering Information:

Prime Seven Media
518 Landmann St.
Tomah City, WI 54660

Printed in the United States of America

TABLE OF CONTENTS

CHAPTER 1

LOIN CAUGHT HIS PREY!

He must make Sam pay for what he has done to him.

He looks at Martha. She became motionless as a statue. Wanting to fight, but how?

Oh, how she feels - like a fool. Letting her father's cousin fool her like this. She wanted to feel as if she were a princess.

It was a game of cat and mouse. Looking around, trying to get the hell out of there.

She didn't know what to do. Wishing that her father could save her. Coming to save the day on his white horse.

Sam's cousin comes in for the kill. Knowing that Martha would give him what he wants.

Martha steps aside. He steps towards her. She looks at him and says, don't you touch me. "I do not permit you to touch me." "My mother told me that no one has permission to touch me." "If I don't say so." A reminder, as pain connected from her arm to her brain.

Sam's cousin looks at her with an evil grin. "I will have your permission soon." While pain, connecting to her cheek. To let her know who was in charge.

"You will help me destroy your father, by my destroying you." "You see, I will take your innocence." "Yes, you will become so dependent on my poison." "I will be the one that will rock your world." "I will take everything from your family. "Then your end will come for you." "Hope will be gone for you." "You won't be worth anything." "NO ONE WILL WANT YOU!" "YOU will join your brother soon."

"See, no one knows you are here." "By the time they know." "You will be gone." "You will be out of the country, and they will never find you." "Martha knew she was in serious trouble."

Deep down within herself. Trying to dig within her soul. Knowing she needs to become in survival mode. To dig out of an evil world, of death.

CHAPTER 2

A NEW DAY

Sam was rolling out of bed. Feeling as if he had conquered the world. Knowing that yesterday was done and over.

Taking a lazy day. With a big breath. Knowing he will hang around the house for a few days. He needs to get his strength back.

Feeling he needs to spend some time with Martha today. He needs to be better in their relationship. He realizes the time you have. Is a gift.

Knowing there is a hole in the heart. He knows it's going to take time. For this hole in the family to heal. This is a loss that he never thought he would have to deal with. He walks out of his bedroom door. Walks down a few doors.

He sees Jean in his son's bedroom. He knows she needed to sleep.

Her hopelessness becomes like an energy vampire sucker. Would take over. He could lose her too. He almost lost her once. She was in the Hospital, for a while. Not wanting to come back to Earth.

He walks by Martha's room just to see if she is still sleeping. He opens her door. Notices that she isn't anywhere.

Where is she? He looks around. Kind of frustrated, he keeps looking, thinking that he could spend some time as a family.

Losing a family member brings perspective into the real world. He knows they need to unite. Just so they could get through this hell here on earth.

Knowing they don't work together. This family will tear apart. Sam knows that the evil one would love to watch. This family to die. This is his goal.

Sam couldn't understand why his cousin hated him so much. He could remember when he was little. How they would get into trouble together. While he goes back in time.

His cousin went on a mission and told Sam. He needed to go on one as well.

Sam would never forget the time when he looked at him. He loved his heavenly Father more than anything. That he needs to tell everyone about his love.

It was because of him he stayed with his Father in Heaven. His cousin is a long way off the beaten path.

While Sam keeps thinking. *How he changed so much. He doesn't understand what happens. How can someone, so fast in a little time? It was only ten and a half years ago that he went on a mission. How could someone know the truth and then deny it?*

How did this happen? Sam's heart is breaking because, for the first time, he is seeing what kind of person his cousin is.

He prayed to him for a long time. Hoping for him to change.

He just lost his son, and now he has just realized it.

His cousin and he were best friends. He has taken his heart and stomped on it. While his cousin doesn't care. They used to be three musketeers. They did everything together.

Terry is his best friend as well. Sam is so thankful to him. *Going back in time; they got in trouble. Some of the stupid stuff they would do. Most of them were not listening to the adults.*

One time. Sam's aunt told them not to slide down the roof. Sam and his cousin and Terry looked at themselves. Having a corky look of relabeling. Waiting for a moment. To do their relabeling.

Heading towards the roof. The roof was a shiny surface. It was a green metal sheet. Knowing they could land on the snow by sliding off the roof. Three of the musketeers. Climbed to the top of the roof.

Not knowing that a corner of the metal sheet. Was bent upward. Ready to slice anything that was to encounter it.

All three got to the top. Getting ready to slide down, to fall into the snowbank. It didn't go as planned. All three of them can remember what happens next. They get to the edge of the peak of this metal roof. Their expectations came to an abrupt end. This slide was going to be exciting, or so they thought.

How the metal corner was going to remind them. To all listen to your aunt. Suddenly, you could hear the cries, of children screaming in pain. As each one went downward, each one got the same mark on their thighs. Each one got remind, of why you should listen to adults.

Sam hasn't thought about that in a long time. He has a half-grin on his face. His aunt has passed away now, but he still has a scar to remind him. While Sam is down memory lane.

Thinking about another time. How they thought it could be a game. To throw a ball over the house without breaking a window. Well, boys will be boys.

The three tried it. Sam's cousin thew the ball first. He barely makes it. Then it was Terry's turn. He had the better arm. He takes the ball. Throws it way over into the neighbor's yard. Hit their car in the carport. Then the window in the driver's seat, shatter. How would they pay for it? Out of their own money. Sam had a half-grin just like he was the Cheshire Cat. With a little chuckle.

Wondering about his cousin.

Does he ever think about the good times, or is he so full of his poison?

What is his story? How can he justify what he has done?

Sam knows he needs to come back to know his Heavenly Father.

As he tries to find Martha, he becomes more frustrated. Knowing that she would have to be somewhere.

He wanted to cook. Breakfast for everyone.

Not knowing at that moment that Martha is in danger.

He needs to get started. Sam was a cook. Before he built his small business, he was in banking.

He made loans all over the world. Even the Pentagon had some of his business. In the business world. His company is famous. He has to trust his employees. Knowing that anyone could use his business to get access. Around the world.

Knowing he must make breakfast, hoping to surprise his family.

He just knows that this would bring Martha out of hiding. He is going to make her favorite breakfast meal.

Martha is in love with biscuits and gravy. He knows that when she smells it. She was coming.

He knows that the only one good thing about buttermilk biscuits. The gravy is oh so nice and hot.

Getting the pots and utensils ready for use. His mind goes back to yesterday.

Sam is feeling like his old self again. Wanting to do some of his pleasures of life and come back to reality.

He knows his son has passed. Yesterday was the day he said his goodbyes.

He couldn't remember much of it. Not knowing where he was. Sam was sure. He saw his cousin there. Not knowing for sure.

Was his cousin there to make trouble for him and his family? He shakes his head to recall. Knowing that he doesn't want to know.

His mind goes back to Martha. Wondering where she was. She had always wanted to help.

He turns off the stove. Just to try one more time to find her. Martha would want to help him make breakfast together. Just so they could be together.

Sam looks again for his little girl. She is nowhere. Sam panicked.

He has a fear swooping over him. Not knowing why? She had to be somewhere. He knows that this feeling isn't going away. Something had to be wrong, but what?

He continues to look for her. Knowing that something isn't right. Knowing that every second would count, just to find her.

As he wanders through the house, calling for her. Hoping to find her.

The butterflies in his stomach were coming to its surface. He goes through frantically looking for his daughter. Where is she?

CHAPTER 3

VISION OF A WARNING

hile red sticky liquid beat through his veins. Gorging them. While heading to the gray world.

He leans against the sofa. Takes a deep breath, hoping to calm his heart rate down enough. *He knows he needs to sit down.*

He needs to find Martha now. *Where is she? Did she go anywhere without saying nothing? The more he worried about her. He couldn't get her out of his mind. If she wasn't there, then where was she?*

Would he be able to find her? Knowing he needed to rest on the sofa for a while. This gray world would hit again if he didn't.

It poured like a stream of water. He knows he still needs to take it easy.

He is the man in the family. Sometimes that meant that he is to keep going at all costs.

He just knows that he is trying to keep it down. It is coming to the surface. The volcano is about to spew its anger and hurt.

All the things that are happening to his family. The worst thing. Is that his little angel goes to his maker? Sam thinks about all of this stuff that is attacking his family, just to destroy it.

Not knowing what the future would be. With his family. Knowing there could be a way. To get back to the way they were. And yet, knowing it will never be the same. It has changed.

Just to know that there is hope. He knows his Heavenly Father. Made families in his image, the way it was in Heaven. Before they came to Earth, families were eternal.

As Sam keeps thinking, *he knows he needs to get off his bottom.*

Back off the sofa. Before he starts breakfast, he needs to find his daughter. It is on his mind, and it will not go away until he does something.

He will continue looking for her. Until he finds her. He just knows something was wrong.

He knew that the gray word would come back. If he overextended, he searched. He just needs to get off the sofa first.

Looking around. Just to see if he could get some help from something. To pull him up.

Noticing Jean's purse, with a piece of paper sticking out of it. Wondering what it is about.

Her boundaries for him. Was important to her. He learns this from his grandmother.

She taught him a lot of things. This was one thing that she taught him.

His mother couldn't teach him. She traveled around a lot in the world. She would be in her own world, but not in reality.

Sam is so curious to know what it is. This piece of paper is calling to him. But he wouldn't touch it. He would wait for his wife to open it.

Then again, she probably already knows what it is all about. Sam tries his best to get to the task at hand.

He just knows that Martha needs to be found and found now. He thinks to himself. *Where would she be?* With this doom in his stomach, now is the time to find her. He needs peace. His family needs to be safe. He needed some quiet thinking.

Everything is going against him. He doesn't seem to get things done. Sam just feels like he has failed everyone around him. He feels. His hope was gone. In this world, was leaving him to fall into a dark hole of hopelessness.

He needs to snap out of it, but darkness stays to eat upon that hope. It is eating away. He knows he has lost his son, now his illness, from his fall. Is taking control. Of his family. This is stopping him from being the strong one. How could he go on and be that?

Strong one? He can't even stand up for very long. Without passing out.

For this thing called the gray world, keeps wanting him to join. This darkness fills his cup and runs over. Ready to take over from him, for his sorrow is too much for him.

He knows that if he doesn't call on his Heavenly Father soon. Doom will take over. Then his family. Could float in the darkness.

He knows that the evil one is waiting to make him pay. While he keeps going on about his weakness now. His body isn't moving.

Contemplating trying to get up again. Knowing that he could see the gray word again. Wondering if he will ever get back to get things done.

Sam decides to just lean back. Just to close his eyes for a moment. Asking his Father in Heaven for help.

Not knowing that he would get a vision. A light came towards him. It is as clear as the sun. While he squints at the bright light.

A bright heavenly messenger came to him. Told him that his daughter, Martha, is in danger as of now. She is in a place of danger. For the evil one has gotten her as of now.

Your father sent me to tell you these things. You need to take heed. If you want to save her.

While Sam becomes kind of confused, a bet. Not quite understanding what this massage is saying. For this massage, would repeat. Knowing he needs to get his strength together now. This message lets him know. You need to save your daughter NOW!

Your Heavenly Father has sent me to tell you. These things, to let you know he sees you. He loves you, and he is with you.

You need to remember that. You will have a lot of heartache if you don't take heed of this warning. Please, you need to understand.

If you don't force yourself up. Then your daughter shell parish. Your Heavenly Father knew this would happen. Before it has. He has given you the tools to accomplish it. Remember, this is a warning. Please take heed of this.

They sent me to give you this message. As this vision was ending, he understood he needed to get it together now.

Sam opens his eyes. Not quite believing. That this angel of warning would come to him. To just warren him of the danger.

To help protect his daughter. After all, Martha was Heavenly Father's daughter first. How would he do this? Where is she? He knows Heavenly Father would know. He knows what to do, was to ask.

CHAPTER 4

DOOM HAS COME!

Meanwhile, Jean came out of the dream world. Noticing that she is on her son's bed.

While she noticed that her son's pillow was a little damp. From the tears of the night before.

Knowing that daytime is here. Her heart broken. She isn't with her son.

Then she remembers the vision that was given to her. This warning that is to happen. She knows she needs to get ahold of Sam and NOW.

Wanting to warn Sam about the dream she had. She did not know that he had just had a warning of his own. She just knows that she needs to save her daughter from the evil one.

First, she needs to go to Martha's bedroom to apologize to her again. The way she treated her.

For this is how Jean's father treated her. She did the same thing. Jean finally notices it. She just did the same thing that her father did to her. The same dysfunctional act. She just knows that she needs to change.

The change is going to come from her. Jean just knows. That everything would have to start with her. Her feeling with her daughter.

She is going to treat her as her little girl. Not as a monster. She needs to treat her as a child of her Heavenly Father, for that is who she is.

A daughter of the Almighty. Jean knows from this vision that she is treating Martha like trash. While she thinks to herself about this. She knows she doesn't deserve her daughter. How dare she treat her daughter like this? She knows it is time to get some help.

Between her childhood and losing her son. It is time. For Jean to admit this, it means one thing. She didn't like to admit what her father had done to her.

She knows she's damaged goods. Her father would let her know this, as a child. She heard this every day for years. Especially when her mother left her all alone with him.

Her mother was sick to the point, for there was no way out. Her mother knew she couldn't beat him and get away from him. Jean just knows that if she doesn't get the help she needs. Either she could do something to herself, or hurt Martha.

She knows that the vision is a warning of what is coming. If she didn't take a head to it. She got up and out of her son's bedroom.

Thinking to herself. *I have failed so much. How am I going to make up for all of this?* She knows that her Heavenly Father would forgive her. But would Martha?

Jean needs to have hope for her daughter's relationship.

She began her journey. Stops at Martha's door. She thinks she is in there.

Wondering why she hasn't opened her door. Trying to understand not to cross boundaries. Wondering if all is well with her, but no answer. Just quiet, nothing.

How can anything get solved if she doesn't open the door? Jean takes a deep breath. Talks to the door. Hoping that Martha would hear her. Still, nothing happens.

Jean got a little frustrated with Martha. She is being a little rude. Frustrated, she heads towards the stairs

Wondering why she didn't talk to her mother.

Jean knows Martha is anger. Who could blame her? Jean blamed Martha for her brother's death.

She steps down onto the last step. Seeing Sam. She could see that he was resting.

Wondering why he is there. Instead of his bed.

Not knowing that he had been up already. Looking for Martha. Know that it looks as if he is still a little weak. Looking as he isn't in this world. Looking pale himself.

She thought maybe Martha would be down here.

Jean thought it would be nice to have breakfast together. Today, she wants to be a close family. She wants to put each other first.

She knows that this family is in danger. The evil one wants to destroy it.

It is time to get that evil one out of their family for good, but how? Jean knows this much. She needs help to get rid of him.

Sam's cousin wants to get even with Sam. Sam will have to get his cousin to leave us alone.

How does he have the way to draw people in, to just take his poison?

CHAPTER 5

A DREAM BECOMES REAL!

*J*ean didn't understand that one. *Her brains go back to where Martha was. She has checked all-round the house and hasn't seen her. Her mind goes back in time. A doom came to her. This has happened before. Her gut is giving the sign to call Lily. Maybe she is with her. Remembering her phone is in her purse.*

She looks towards her purse. Knowing that it is at the end of the table, by the sofa.

She heads toward the living room. Where the sofa is. Noticing a piece of paper sticking out. *Wondering what it is about.*

Her curiosity got the better of her. Never having seen it before. Jean gets closer to the piece of paper with every step.

Her stomach jumps around. Knowing that something isn't right. That isn't ever a good sign for her.

Her heart is beating so fast. That her veins were filling with red sticky liquid. She just knows this will not be good.

She finally gets there. Reach outward for the piece of paper. Not knowing what it said. She opens it slowly, as it makes a crinkling sound.

Knowing this note will give her some kind of information. She didn't know what it would tell her. Her heart skip. The tune of her heart beating.

She knows that something didn't feel right. She opens it, wondering. If it was bad news. While she walks over to the sofa. She opens it; she reads...

"Mother, I am down in the city with Dad." "Don't worry, I am fine." "I am going to be in the farmer's market area." "Father and I will be home as soon as we can. Bye. Jean sees this; her red sticky liquid boils. She knew who had her.

Sam couldn't have taken her to the city. He is here beside her on the sofa. She knows that either Sam's cousin is involved or she left herself.

Jean knows that the dream she had was coming true. This is going to be a rescue mission for her daughter.

She knows that Sam isn't going to do much. Knowing that he is still so weak.

She woke him anyway. She knew he would be a very upset person if she didn't. Knowing that there is doom in the air for her daughter.

CHAPTER 6

PLAN FOR A RESCUE

Jean knows that she would have to call some people for help. This note put fear in her heart. This vision she had was starting.

She knows that she can't do it on her own. It is time to call for help. For Martha is in danger with the evil one.

Jean leans over to wake Sam up. To let him know what is going on, and what they are going to deal with. His cousin is the problem.

Jean knows it is time to make some phone calls now. She hands Sam the phone.

Not knowing why, she handed him the phone. Sam is still trying to wake up. He was still in a daze.

Jean looked at him and says, Call Terry. "Martha is in danger." "We need to find her, NOW."

Sam looked at Jean with a confused look. Still half asleep, and not knowing what just happened. Jean scooted over. Just to let him read the note himself. Sam reads it, and for the first time. His heart told on him. Knowing his vision is happening

He has to choose. It is his daughter or cousin. All the hurt that his cousin has done, and his heart breaks.

He knows without a doubt who it would be-his daughter. He needed to kick some butt. Would he have enough strength?

Sam wondered how he would get it. He looks at Jean. He asks, "Who did you call." "I have called no one yet", as she answers.

She looks back at Sam. Just to let him know that he needs to call Terry right NOW. Then, I will call the police. Just to get them there quicker.

Ask Terry to come over to pick you up. I will call Emmaline. To see if she could take me there.

You and I need to save our daughter and family. We have to work together or lose our family. I saw this in a vision. While she looks at in the eyes. How it ends is up to us. I need your help, Sam. Are you with me? Because if you won't be.

Let me know. Martha is our daughter, and we need to save her NOW. Are you in? Sam looks at Jean with a look of admiration.

Sam loves it when Jean takes charge. He loved watching a female in charge. Sam felt as if he just might like Jean going after his cousin. He knows that Jean is going to hurt his cousin, and hurt him horribly. When she sees him. He'd better look out for her. The mother is here to protect her child. Be careful; the mother bear is on the loose. He loves it when she gets protective. She would come alive.

Most of the time. She was so calm that people would just step on her, then walk away. Not knowing what kind of damage. They would leave behind.

Sam just knows this is different. This is about the maternal instinct.

Jean is in charge, as if she were a bull. Getting ready to charge, anything in the way. Knowing that she could hurt anything in her path.

Her goal is to get her daughter at any cost, safe. She continues to look at Sam. Just to let him know that she is willing to do anything. Just to make sure that Martha is safe. Jean didn't know exactly what to do.

She knew that she had her gun with her. Being willing to use it if she had to.

Sam didn't like it when she had the gun.

Jean keeps on looking and talking to Sam, letting him know that he needs to call Terry now.

They need to get to the farmer's market now. Sam agrees that he needs to get there. Just to save her, hoping that she would be safe and sound. Waiting for her father.

Sam prayed to himself. Knowing that she is in danger with his cousin. He knows that it is a matter of time. It is here.

He knows the consequences of turning his cousin in. Will have his reward from his cousin.

Sam knew that it was his actions that would cause Martha pain. His cousin always told him, "You will pay." Sam knew what better way than his daughter. Thinks to himself. *If you want to get even with the parent, get the child.*

This is what his cousin is doing. Sam knew that he needed to pick up the phone and start calling.

Hoping that Terry would pick up the phone.

Knowing that he could be sleeping. He hates bothering him. When he is in bed. He has been there to help in so many ways already. Now, Sam has to call him one more time for help.

Sam hates to ask for help, but he is still weak from the loss of red sticky liquid. He knows that he is still quite dizzy. From the lack of it.

He hears it ringing. It rings for the second time. No answer.

His heart beat faster. It is filling his veins with the pressure of the red sticky liquid. Pumping through his veins to his heart.

As his brain tries to go to the gray world again. Sam knows what is coming. He has been there a few times in the last twenty-four hours.

Sam tries his best to fight it. Not wanting to lose the battle. He needs to fight for his daughter. Which he needs to fight against his cousin.

How could he do this? He can't even stand at these times. Not without falling.

While he keeps listening to the ringing. Wondering if he will pick up. It rings two more times. Then Terry answer. "Hello",

"Sam, are you good." "Do you need me for something?" Sam answers back. "We have a note that Martha is in the city."

"We are heading there." "Could you join us." "We will be at the Farmers Market." "I am thinking somewhere in the homeless area." Terry asks him, "Why there?"

"That is where my cousin sells his poison." "Could I get your help." "I can't do this all by myself." "I am bringing my gun just in case something happens, and I need to use it."

For the first time, Terry realizes that Sam is done with his cousin. And his heart sank.

Terry asks Sam, "Where do we meet?"

Sam sighs while his heart beats to the tune of a drum.

While Terry asks him again. Not knowing that Sam still wants to go back to the gray world.

Finley Sam answers him back. "I am fine."

"Could you come here?" "Yes, I could, said Terry. "I will be there in ten minutes". Then, he hung up the phone.

Then Sam waits. Grayness is coming again.

Then Jean got ahold of Emmaline. "Told her about the note in her purse." "That Martha put it there to let me know where she was." Emmaline asks her, "What did it say?" Jean says it says that she was meeting her father in the city — going to meet him at the Farmers Market." "Sam is next to me.

Emmaline isn't too shocked. She knew who was behind this. She asks, "Do you know who did it? Jean answers, "Yes."

Emmaline answers back, "Let me guess who." Jean says, "You're right." "It is he again, Sam's evil cousin." "Could you come here first?"

"I knew that it would take two hours for you to get here." "I have called the police already." "They are on their way here." "To get a photo of her and make a report out."

"Meanwhile, they will look for her as well."

"Emmaline, I pray that everything will be good."

As Emmaline gets into her car, she keeps talking to Jean. Knowing that Jean could be close to losing it.

Jean buried her son yesterday, and her daughter took off with an evil man. How is she coping? Knowing the worst could happen.

Emmaline knows that Jean could snap easily. As she pulled out, she was still on the phone with Jean. Wondering if she is good.

Knowing that she would have to pay attention on the road. Knowing that she would have let go of the phone.

Emmaline telling Jean. She would pick her up at the house. To be ready for the city.

Jean just knows that Sam's cousin is a dangerous person. Not knowing what he would do to Jean's daughter.

Jean got her gun ready to use. While she put it in her purse,

Emmaline is praying to the Heavenly Father most of the way to Jean's house.

She knew this was going to be dangerous. Sam's cousin could do anything to keep Martha as his trophy. Martha is young and beautiful. Emmaline just knew this was a matter of life and death.

He could traffic her to anyone. Her innocent beauty is attractive to the opposite sex. This is what Sam's cousin does. To sell his poison.

He needed to get even with Sam. Anyone who is around Sam will pay for his revenge. Jean just knew that this couldn't last very long.

Knowing that once, he gets Martha involved in sex trafficking. It would be impossible to find her.

CHAPTER 7

A RACE TO SAVE.

*J*ean knew her daughter was in danger. The only thing that could save her. Is for her to get on her knees. Pleading before her Heavenly Father for mercy. The agony she was in, brought in these scriptures. Into her mind. *In Matthew 18:20 it says, for where two or three are gathered together in my name, there I am in the midst of them.* Jean remembers this verse from church.

She knew that Emmaline and she needed to pray to find Martha. If they are to have any hope of finding her.

Jean knew that she needed to grab her gun, hoping not to use it. She knows that it is better to be safe than sorry.

She knew that Emmaline doesn't like guns, and she won't tell her until the right time.

That time would be at the time her daughter was in danger.

She would do anything for her daughter to be safe. She can blame her daughter for her son's death, but no one else put Martha in danger. Jean will become ballistic with them. This is her little girl, and no one will hurt her.

Jean knows where the gun is. Upstairs in her closet. On the top shelf, where her hats were. Her bullets were in her dresser, where her underwear was. Thinking back in time.

She made sure that the chamber was loaded correctly.

Jean had known how to use a gun since she was a teen. Her grandpa, her mother's dad. Taught her how. Her grandpa didn't like her father and knew what he did. The law protected him. Her grandpa was a farmer, and he knew how to shoot. Jean knew the story.

He was in Word War 2 vet. Her grandpa would come back from the war. Then go back to the farm. His parents had.

It was years later that my mother's. Got married to father.

As she keeps trying to think about other things to keep her from thinking about Martha.

This is crazy. She is going to drive herself nuts by the time Emmaline gets here.

Jean knows that the carpet will thin out soon. By walking back and forth. While she chews on her nails. Hoping and praying with every step. That Sam's cousin doesn't hurt Martha.

The thoughts of Grandpa aren't working anymore. Her mind is on her daughter.

While she keeps pacing back and forth. Waiting for Emmaline to show up. As she is doing this, Sam is still having some problems. With his head beating to a tune. Hard enough that he is holding his head. Sam needs to be ready to be picked up by Terry.

CHAPTER 8

A MOTHER'S PAIN!

Jean is also waiting for the police officer. To show up. To have a report done on Martha. She knew that the sooner the report is done. The sooner Martha would be safe.

Jean really wanted Martha in her arms. In her arms, safe and warm. She is a mother, that lost her son. Now, it could be her daughter next. Looks at the heavens.

"I am a mother that could be Mother-less." "Within two days." "She takes her fist and shakes it toward the heavens."

"Then tell me, Heavenly Father, with all of her anger, why?" "My heart is breaking for my son and NOW. My daughter is in danger.

"You let an evil man take her, to hurt her." "I am anger with you." "How could you do this." "To an innocent child." "Why do you let people hurt the innocent children?" "Why can't you stop them?"

Then her Heavenly Father told her in her mind and heart, with a peace in her. Can't go past the agency. I respect it so much. He tells her.

"I cannot make them do the right thing, or love their brethren." "Their hearts are far from me, and their hearts have hardened

Towards me." "Daughter, I am with you, but I can't do that." "I will be here."

"Watching and working with the innocent to heal, and learning from it."

"To turn to me for hope, for miracles to happen." "Your daughter will hurt, but it will not define her." "You will find her." "She will be good." "Remember the vision you had, claim the promise." "I will be there." "It is okay to be angry with me." "Just don't turn away from me." "I can take the anger." "I understand, but there is a plan for your family." "Hold sight to that." "You will need to go through all of this." "To get the blessing, that I have for your family." "Remember this."

It left just as fast as it had come. Jean is alone again. She has peace within herself. Not on pins and needles. She just knows that everything would be good.

Now that her Heavenly Father is in control of it all. While she keeps walking back and forth with ease.

There was a knock at the door. It is a police officer. He is there to take a report of another missing child. Children are missing from so many small towns. Even their large cities have gone up in small children and teens vanished.

He is asking for a picture of her. Looking at it, thinking about her innocence.

Then he asks Jean, where could she be? Jean knows where she is. With one look, he knew. He will find out. He looks at her again.

Then he asks for the evidence. Jean hands over the note. That Martha left. That would tell them where she would be.

As the police officer looked at it, he noticed. With his hand on his forehead, rubbing in frustration. It is in the area where the homeless is. With a look that said it all. Right in the area were multiple girls and boys who disappeared. This is the area of the warning. They have an investigation going on in that area.

The F.B.I. is involved. Knowing that he needed to call in pronto. That this girl could be in danger. Asking Jean to stay there. Not wanting her in the action. Knowing that there could be people. Have their light leave their eyes. Not knowing for sure whether Martha would come home. Wondering if they could find her, already gone to another world.

This police officer was trying his best not to let it show, for this was his job. That they would find her and be ready to pick her up at the station. She looks at the police officer just to let him know that Sam and Terry are on their way.

The police officer says, "I will put out an A.P.B. for her." "You will hear from us." "Mrs. We will find her." "Remember, you need to stay here." "I'll call you." With a look of concern. "We know where this is." "We have been checking this place out for a while."

"If we don't act, know." "Your daughter's lost forever." "If you go down there." "It could blow all of our time on our investigation, sex trafficking in the city." "It is one of the biggest crimes in the United States and the world." "Few of the guys have been praying for us to find it and shut it down in our city." "This could be the answer to our prayers." "I know a mother's love wants to tear a-part the predator." "Please let us do our job." "We need to stop them." "Please stay here."

Jean walks with him. Open the door for him. Knowing that he is so right about going down there. It could start trouble. Sam's cousin needs to pay.

She is becoming an animal. She wishes the evil one would die. A painful death. While watching him, have the light leave his eyes. Trying not to say a word of her thoughts.

As he walks out the door, he gives her a card. With his number on it. He looks at her and tells her. "Call me when you have a question." "I will work on this." "You know that you're." "Daughter isn't the only one." "There has been a child missing every few days." "We know where they go." "We just can't prove it." "The law isn't fair to the victims."

"Please stay away from there." "We need to get this group of evil men and women." "Get the proof that will put them away or their light from their eyes." "Will fade away." "We know that it will just take a little more time." "More time for more victims."

"Meanwhile, your daughter's case." "I will be the first one to work on this." "All I can do is tell you." "We are in this department." "We are working night and day on this case." "I know that this isn't much comfort." "Just remember that you're not the only parent who has a child missing." "We will find her."

As he walks out the door, walking down the sidewalk. Shaking his head. While heading toward his car. Talking on his radio. Letting them know about another child missing.

Jean shut her front door. With her head downward, as if she has the entire world on her shoulder. Walking over to her big picture window. Watching him talk on his radio. Wondering when Emmaline would get there.

She should get there soon. Let Emmaline know what the police officer said. "That they need to stay at the house." "Wait for their call." "When they find her." "We could go to the station and pick her up."

Jean's energy vampire sucker is pecking through. Heads to the gray—world again. It is making its way back. Just as it plays peek-a-boo. With her low.

She was thankful that it took a break for a while. Jean knew what her Heavenly Father told her. He warned her about the darkness.

How it would bring her to her knees. He will give her power. Just when she is thinking of giving in. Help will come to her. To help grow into that goddess. She could be. Jean was back in her thoughts about this dream.

Emmaline pulls into the driveway. Jean is so relieved. She knows that she needs to remember what was told to her. She needed to have hope again.

Emmaline grabs her purse from the passages' seat. Making sure she gets her keys. Since she always seems to forget them. Head for the front door. While knowing why she is there. Her heart swelled with fear for Martha.

CHAPTER 9

WANTING TO PUT A STOP TO EVIL!

*J*ean told her what the police officer said and took a report. Took a picture of Martha. She also told Emmaline that there were at least two children missing every week.

She continues to look at her and said, "This is heartbreaking." "There are parents like me." "That are going through hell as well." "This needs to stop." "How can this happen?" Being taken away from their home." "To be sold for slaves for some sick adult pleasure - this is wrong on so many levels."

Jean continues to look at Emmaline. Not understanding. Why haven't they been able to put a stop to it? "Too many children sacrificed." "If there is only one, that is too much." While she took her fist and hit the top of the table. Knowing pain rushes to the brain. Showing her feeling.

You could tell that her blood was coming to a boiling point. Her veins on her forehead are popping out. This is a way for people to know.

She is angry. To get away from her. Then you are safe.

Jean needs to calm down. While she is weaving back and forth. Acting as if she is going. To a gray-world. Reality is setting in.

It is as if she isn't getting any air. She needed to sit down. It is as if her heart could beat out of chest. Then she had the chills.

She needs to calm herself. She thinks to herself. *Her daughter's missing had brought all this on her.*

Jean isn't doing well. Having her heart ripped out of her chest, and cut to pieces. She just wished that she could tell Martha. She was so sorry for blaming her for her brother's death.

If she could just do that. This whole thing with Sam's cousin might not have happened. If she would just love her more and not be so mean to her.

She looked at Emmaline and spoke. "I need to do better than this." "I can't keep doing this to Martha." "It has to stop." "Emmaline, I need help." "What do I do to get it?" Emmaline just looks at her. "I will see what I can do to get you someone."

"Now what are we going to do?" "Are we going to get Martha or what?" Jean just looks at her for a few minutes. Just leaving Emmaline wondering what is going on. She didn't know exactly. She knew nothing had happened. With the police yet. Making a missing person report.

Emmaline looked at Jean and asked her what he said. Jean answered. "He told me to stay here." "Not to go down there." "To stay out of the way." "That they will call when they find her."

Jean continues to look at Emmaline. Wondering if this is the right thing to do. Jean continues looking at her. While asking if she should go down and kick somebody's butt. Namely, Sam's cousin.

If she could just have a moment with him. She knows that with one pull of a trigger. Just one tiny mental bullet. Would do the job. She could get rid of him.

Jean is trying to be a Christian lady. Wanting to do the right thing, she wants him badly. To just pay for what has been done.

Her bitterness is growing. In time, it will become a monster that could destroy her. It needed to be stopped beforehand.

She knows that if she didn't control it now. It will eat away at herself. This really would destroy her family. As she keeps wondering, how do I stop this? No one knows where I come from.

Some of this stuff that happens. Just happens, and I can't stop it. While she puts her hand on her forehead. While Emmaline could see her face. It shows her disappointed look.

Emmaline could tell that she is heading into the darkness. Emmaline knows that she needs to pull her out before she gets in too deep.

Once she gets deep in that gray world. It becomes impossible. To get her back to Earth.

Emmaline knows that Jean should be on medication. It would help her, but for now. She knows that she needs to be there to help.

She also knows that the police officer is right. Jean wouldn't be able to handle it. Even thou she agrees. With what Jeans is saying. Sam's cousin should not have his hand slapped anymore. His life should end.

Emmaline already knows that with Sam and Terry going over there, it will be enough trouble. She just knows that Sam had brought his gun.

She is going to be surprise, if Sam is calm enough not to use it on his cousin.

He knows that it is his job to protect his little girl.

While her thoughts go back to Jean. Knowing what could happen to her. If she watches out for herself. Not worrying about Martha, she can't help her.

Emmaline wondered if Sam and Terry had made it yet. If there is a shootout, with Sam's cousin. Knowing that Sam or his cousin could get hurt, or worse yet, Martha

Not knowing what might happen next. She knows that Jean is safe. Is Martha safe?

Emmaline sank. Her trying not to show it. She knows this could go badly. She has dealt with clients. That has come from sex trafficking.

How she tries to help them. Most of the clients do well and have good lives. Then some never recover. Emmaline is thankful for the ones that do. She doesn't understand why someone would do this to an innocent child. Why would they want to? Why would a mature man or woman do this to an innocent girl or boy?

While she keeps thinking about these things that are going on. Jean is watching her and knows without a doubt; it is about Martha.

Jean also wondered if Sam and Terry got there. Knowing they headed out a few hours ago.

Jean talked to Emmaline. How her blood is boiling and why this is happening to them. While she knows the danger that her loved ones are in. All because of one person. How their lives could be in danger.

That she knows that she isn't strong enough to do this.

Telling Emmaline that she has a gun in her purse. That she would like to use it on Sam's cousin. Her feeling about him and how he needs to die NOW. While Emmaline steps backward.

Jean thinks that a person who hurts a child for his benefit. Then just throw them away, just like you would throw your trash out. She looks at Emmaline again. Just to let her know that she meant what she said.

"Another thing that pisses me off." "It is that. They get away with it and continue on their evil way." "Then do it again, over and over."

"Just like they didn't get right the first time, or get enough of their victims." "Even better yet, they cry out that they are the victims."

Jean looks at Emmaline and makes a fist. Slams against the sofa. While she hits it. She screams in pain for her daughter. While she was reacting to her agony. Going over the same heartbreak. The darkness is repeating itself.

That she doesn't know if she will see her for a while. "I am so tired of people getting away with evil deeds." "People hurt innocent children, for the children are the ones that pay."

"Why is it that evil people get the law on their side." "The innocent suffers the heartache." "That has them for the rest of their lives." "It just doesn't end for them." "It is only the beginning." "I don't understand this. "The law gives the predator the okay." "To hurt and maim the innocent, and the law will protect them."

Jean becomes angrier about the laws. Knowing that she is right. The law doesn't work for the innocent anymore. Jean tries to keep going on about the law. The more she talks about it, the hotter her blood boils.

CHAPTER 10

WANTING A PHONE CALL

Emmaline tries to take her mind off Sam and Terry. It didn't work. Once, Jean had one thing on her mind. Everyone is going to know.

Jean keeps walking back and forth, wondering what is going on with Sam and Terry. Neither of them has heard anything from them. What is happening? Thinking the worst thing ever.

Did Sam's cousin get the best of them and just wait to come and get Jean, as she thinks to herself? Just knowing that Sam's cousin came over there to hurt or maybe even kill them both. Just to get even with Sam.

While she slips some of her thought out of her mind. Emmaline thought that she needed to stop and take a chill pill. Just so she could put something else into her brain. It is even too much for Emmaline.

Jean is driving Emmaline away with her thoughts. Emmaline keeps having wild thought of her own. Going through her brain.

Yet Jean keeps a fast pace of walking back and forth. Knowing that time is ticking away. She is becoming very inpatient. She wants to know now. What is going on with her husband, daughter, and Terry?

Jean has a problem. She has never enjoyed being left in the dark, of not knowing.

Waiting for Sam to call. In the pit of her stomach, something had gone wrong. This isn't normal. When Sam left, he said he would call. Jean just wouldn't stop. Panic has grabbed her. Deep down in herself.

Emmaline wants to run up the wall. Just to get away. She just remembered the sleeping pills that Sam had.

Oh, peace would have been so nice, *so she thinks. Emmaline wishes upon a dream at this moment.* She knows that this could last for several hours. It is around noon.

Emmaline tried her best to settle down Jean. She tries to get Jean to eat some lunch.

Knowing that she needs to take some medication. That could help with her anxiety, for it is acting up again.

Emmaline knows the sign. She has them as well. Not as bad. She could tell also because Jean's breathing is deep. She couldn't speak clearly. That is a clue about Jean.

Emmaline decided that they both need to eat something.

Know that it probably would be better to warm leftovers from the refrigerator. Now, with some of the food from the funeral gone.

She is so thankful that the church lady made the food. Knowing that they both need to eat something. Knowing this will be the best way to get her medication into her.

Jean is still pacing the floor. Wearing the rug out. She is walking back and forth. Worrying about her daughter. Knowing at this moment, it is her fault.

She chased her daughter to get her to do this. With each step. She prays that she is safe. Knowing that it is going to take a miracle. She knows who could give that miracle. Asking her Heavenly Father for understanding.

This energy vampire, Sucker, would always seek her out. Just to eat off of her. To dry her out. No hope, no faith. It will drag her down into a world with no hope.

Just to end her reign in her family.

She remembers the vision she had. It is like a whisper in her ear. Just to remind her of what she saw.

She did not deny what she had seen. Knows that her Heavenly Father knew it. She did too.

Now, it is time to believe it. To believe it enough to stop what she is doing. Just having the hope, then doing the action. Then leave it there. Have faith in Heavenly Father to do his job. Jean knows that this is what she has to do. If she doesn't, she could end up back in the old gray world again.

How would she get out to save her daughter? She knows that she can't save her.

Jean knows that she needs to stop walking back and forth. That it is time to lay it in the Heavenly Father's hand. No more fighting. She let him know. There is nothing he can't do.

She stops walking back and forth. She continues to stand there. Taking her arms, as if she is carrying something. Suddenly, she takes her arms and throws them downward. Just like she is acting angry, as if she is two years old. Having a fit. Just to show her Heavenly Father. That she gives it to him.

As she did, her body was overcome with peace. She felt arms wrapping around her with love. Like she had never known before.

She falls to knees. Knowing that he is going to take care of it.

Her vision is going to happen. She knows that her Heavenly Father. Giving her a warning of what is coming.

Just to have her humble herself before him. Knowing he can work on giving blessing. He knows everyone in this family.

Jean knows this. Each one is different, but together they form a whole. It is a family.

It is time we acted like it. She is becoming a new woman.

With hope for the future. Knowing that, the vision. Was a warning for her family.

She took a deep breath. Knowing that she needs to start anew. How does that work? She didn't know. She realizes for the first time. Her eyes have become open.

CHAPTER 11

SEARCHING FRANTICALLY

Meanwhile, Sam and Terry got down to the farmers' market. They looked for Martha. Wondering if they could find her before a bad thing would happen.

Knowing that Sam's cousin is with her. Knowing that with his evil ways. Martha isn't safe. Frantically, Sam becomes scared for her.

Sam still wanted to head to the gray world. He has to stop every once in a while. Just to slow it down. Stopping the grayness is impossible. Sam would have to stop and sit for a few minutes. He would take deep breaths. Trying his best to chase it away. He wonders if it is going to take over.

He knows that if he would just stop, pray for faith to turn to hope. Hope become miracles.

Sam knows that he will still have to work for it. He has to take action. If he sits around expecting to do nothing. There wouldn't be anything done.

He knows that his daughter's miracle will not happen.

Sitting down on a box crate. He needs to get up. With his legs wobbling, it is as if they would collapse.

He leans toward the trash bin. All sudden, Lily comes down the alley. Looking for Martha, hoping to find her.

Lily just watches him. Realizing that, Sam. *With the loss of his red sticky liquid. The day before. This made him weaker than normal.*

She watches him. Just trying to make sure that he doesn't get lost, either. Knowing that he could do that easily. She also knows that Sam will not let this go. Sam didn't just quiet; that wasn't him. Lily looks at Sam and asks him. "What can I do to help?" Sam looked at her back and said, "I need to find my daughter." "Before my cousin hurt her". "Please could you help me find her? "

With sadness in his eyes. She knows his heart is breaking. Her heart goes out to him. She thinks to herself as she begins a quiet pray for him. *As she says, "Dear Heavenly Father", this family needs your guidance and love." "You are the only one that can do a miracle here". "In this family". "You know they have already lost one child'. "Please don't let them lose another". "Please keep Martha safe from Sam's cousin". "Let nothing come to her that will harm her". "Martha will need your help her, and Sam also". Please help them." With a thought to end.*

Knowing that they will find her soon. Lily monitors Sam. Sam knew that he might not keep going.

Shows Lily his gun. Lily understands why. He wasn't okay with it. Knowing he had a permit. Lily knew that this could cause a big problem. Even if Sam was legal.

Looking at shooting a predator. Would be against the law. The law still would have a problem with it. Lily looked at Sam and said,

"I understand why, but you can get in trouble for this. Sam knows she is right.

He looks at her, knowing his rational thinking is gone . He will take his cousin's life for his daughter's. Say that he is sorry. That he will do anything to save her.

Sam is still having problems. With him fading into the gray world. Lily knew that he would head to another world soon. While Sam leans against the garbage bin. Lily continues talking to him. With a soft and gently voice. She bends in closer to him. Trying to hear him.

His voice became so soft she couldn't hear it.

She knows that he needs to go back to the house. She knows that he would not go for that.

This is about his daughter. He is her father. Just to protect her.

As she gets her cell phone, a man in a uniform. Came up to Lily. Wondering if he could help. Lily looked at him and said, "yes". "I need to get him to my car." "Could you help me do that, please? "As she gives him a confuse, look.

While the officer helps her. She asks him if there is a report done on a missing child. The officer looks at Lily. Asking her, what missing report are you talking about?

Lily kind of stepped back. As she looked at him, and spoke. "We have a missing person." "His daughter came down here." "We are pretty sure." "It could be an abduction." "She is only eleven years old."

The officer looks at her. Knowing that this could be dangers for the Elven year-old girl.

He did not know who she was, but it broke his heart. Most of the girls and boys who, they have taken. Knowing what he sees every day. Finding a body with poison in it. The ages run between two and up.

Just to think that she could be in danger. This area that they are in. It is very dangers for young girls. This would have been the place where they would have disappeared. He also knows that they suspected that somewhere in this area is a sex trafficking ring. That they have been trying to close for some time. He knows that he needs to check on this immediately. His gut is telling him this isn't good.

He tries his best to help Lily with Sam. Just to get him back to the truck safely. Knowing that every moment, this woman is in danger. Not knowing that Lily could take care of herself. It is Martha who is in danger.

He definitely needs to get back to his squad car. The officer needs to check in about the report, then see if they can get some officers to check the area for a missing person.

He knows that first he needs to tell Lily to stay back. Not knowing that she worked in the army in Afghanistan. Lily told the officer that she had been in combat before.

She has known how to take care of herself and everyone around her. The officer looked at her and said, "What kind of combat have you been in? "Lily looked at him and said, "I was in Afghanistan, and fought the Taliban". "I have seen the worst. He looks at her. Not knowing what to say to her.

Thinking that she is just a bossy stay-at-home parent. Not knowing that she fought for our freedom. He looks at her and said, "Thank you for fighting for our freedom." "I know that you want to help, but if I let you help." "It could jeopardize you or the girl that is in danger." "I will get some officers together." "To search the area." "You need to stay with him." "If we find nothing." "I will put an eye out personally." "What's her name?"

"I have been investigating this sex trafficking for a while." "I know that it is in this area." Lily looked at him and said, "How do you know, and why are you telling me this?" The officer looks at her. "I am telling this so you can take care of him." "Then I can do my job." "I also might need your help sometime."

"You have seen dead bodies, right?" "I know military personnel stick together." "I know I was Army." "We have a code for each other." "Still live with this code today." "Never leave a brother or sister down."

"Might need you to help save the little girl. "As of now, I need you to stay with him". "I will be back to see if you are okay".

"I might need your help if we find her." He still looks at her in the eye. "We might not find her for a few days." "We will do our best." As he looks into eyes, "Make sure I know where you are."

Lily knew that he meant business. She looks at and grins. Knowing that she could be in trouble. If she is to interfere with police work. This would be bad for her.

He seems to want to help. Lily knows from experience, as a military veteran. She is no longer to serve as a member of the Military Police. She knows these days are over. Oh boy, she wants to be part of the action.

Martha reminded her of the little girl she had lost. This time, she is in danger. She thinks to self. *Does Martha even know how dangerous this is? Is she with Sam's cousin? Has he even hurt her yet? She knows that she can't leave Sam yet. She would have to leave him in the truck.*

CHAPTER 12

DESPERATELY SEARCHING!

While she would go snooping around. Making sure she would ask questions. *Just to see if anyone saw her. Would people even talk to her? She didn't look like an officer. Not anymore, she thought. Lily could see the harm that the poison could do. They are taking and killing them in so many ways. The more she saw.*

She remembers she had a picture of Martha. She knows that she can use this. Just to see if people have seen her.

As she takes it out of wallet, she drops her keys. Hoping they wouldn't fall down the hole where the water drains off the road. On the side of the sidewalk.

As it misses the hole, she dumps her purse. Know that there are people watching her.

Wondering if Martha could be there. In the crowd. As she picks up the thing, watching the crowd for her. *She is trying not to think about what could happen to her. Lily always tries to think positively. This helps her in her line of work. When she was a Military Police. She would always try to investigate with a positive attitude.*

Lily needs to remember she is not a military police investigator anymore.

She will use the same tools. To find a little girl. Just find out what happens to her.

The officer told her to stay put. This wasn't Lily. She is a person. That wants to right the wrongs that are being done. On the innocent. Especially the young ones.

The first thing to do. Sam needs to be in the truck, safe. She knows he is dozing in and out of the gray world. Not knowing where he is.

Lily knows that he is trying so hard to protect his little girl. She knows he is failing. It is up to Terry and her to find her.

She first calls Terry on the cell phone to make sure he is still around the area.

Just to see if he could help Sam. Deep down, she knows she would do a better job. Finding Martha, then Sam.

Lily is what they called the finder. She is always called in to find someone.

Lily knows from the experience, this was dangers. If Sam's cousin is in the business of sex trafficking. Then this is dangers.

Martha could dead. With the poison they would give her. The evils of bad people, that choose to do evil.

Therefore, Lily quit being a Military Police. There is too much evil in the world. To her, she would get one bad person, and then another would come along. She knows that she needs to call Terry now. Just to find out where he is.

CHAPTER 19

FINDING A PLACE OF EVIL

hile she digs for his cell phone in his pocket. She notices Sam's gun. *She thinks to self, why would he be needing it for safety reasons?*

Not knowing what could happen to Sam.

Lily finding Sam's phone. She dials Terry's cell number. Wondering if he would answer. She knows how he hates the phone and doesn't like to talk.

Lily could hear the phone ring twice. Then, Terry picks up the phone and starts talking.

Knowing that it is Lily. "Hey honey, did you find anything on Martha? "Lily answered him right back. "No, "I didn't". "I need you to come over here". "Watch the truck and watch Sam." Terry was a little reluctant. Not wanting to leave his area.

He knows that Sam isn't doing very well. He also knows that Lily could get farther than he would. She knows how to look.

He knows that Sam would want to kill people. Just to find his little girl. Anyone who would stand in his way. He would cut them down.

Just to save a child. He learned how to do that in the army. To him, that would be a sacrifice. Lily has done this for her country as well. She would know what to do. Terry knows what would be best. Sam needs to go to the truck. Just like Lily asked him to do. Knowing that he wants to be the one to find Martha. He won't be a hero to Martha. Knowing that he would be the hero for Sam's cousin. This is what he wants.

Lily will have to find Martha. Terry headed back towards the truck, praying that Lily would find Martha safe.

He is walking past an old car detailing shop. Something didn't seem right. His heart acts as if it is going to leap out of his chest. His stomach acted up. It seemed to him he is going to get sick. He couldn't understand why he was feeling so poor suddenly.

As he continues walking, passed the car dealership. Terry could see some kind of activity, but didn't pay any attention to it. He goes down further. Terry looks over and notices. He is feeling pretty good at this moment.

Why, he feels sick, and now he is feeling good? He wondered why? He thinks of going back. Just to wonder if his Heavenly Father is telling him something. This evil place is here. Terry turns around. He sees a couple of men looking at him. Noticing this feeling of doom. He could feel the icy stare of evil. It became as if they could stare a hole through him.

His hair at the back of his neck stood up. He knows there is evil at that car dealership. He needs to get to Lily now. To use the phone to call the officer. Just to check out the place. He knows that Martha has to be in there. Just a feeling.

As he walks fast towards the truck, he sees people strung out.

Hanging on the sidewalk. Dying from the poison they have taken.

Knowing that Sam's cousin is sailing this stuff. He has been after Martha for some time. As he keeps looking, he notices people. Strung out as well.

Probably thinking this is the way to live. That this poison is killing them slowly. Knowing they don't know any better. While his heart sank, they died slowly.

Terry, knowing that he needs to get himself over there fast. He picks up speed. Lily needs to know.

Looking at the evil place. He thinks he knows where Martha is. Just need to find a way of getting in there. To get her out. His heart leaps. He knows that Lily would know how. To get in. She has done this before. Get in and out as if she were a ghost.

She did this kind a stuff for the United States. She would know how to do this. Without their knowing it.

Terry knows that Martha would be in safer hands. He needs to get there fast and now. He knows that they would sell her if they knew of a rescue.

This family needs to survive.

Terry picks up speed faster than before. In, out, and around people. Looking back every few seconds. Just to make sure he is not being followed. Noticing that they were watching him.

Those men are there to intimidate anyone who comes onto their property. He knows there is an evil thing going on there, but does not know what? The feeling of evil is very strong. He can see the truck finely. He sees Lily bringing Sam.

Noticing that Sam didn't look very well. Terry knows he would watch over him. He would stay to watch over him.

First, he needs to talk to Lily. About what he saw. Knowing what she needs to know.

They will need to get hold of the officers. They had talked to earlier that day.

Still not understanding a lot of the stuff that is happening. He gets to the truck. See Lily; tell her what he has experienced. Lily has become excited as she looks at Terry. Just to let him know, he did it. Terry looked at Lily and said. "Did what"? "You found the sex trafficking ring. That has been in our town.

"Don't you see." "This is where Martha must be, and the sex trafficking ring as well."

"We need to get ahold of the officer, and now." "You need to stay here." "You call the officer; here is his number." "Tell him where I am." Terry looks at her. "You can't go." "This isn't safe."

Lily looks at him. "You know that I'm the only one who can do this." "I am qualified for this." "You know that I am right." Terry looks at her. *He knows that she is so right. This is what she did for the military. She would put her life in danger every day for our freedom.*

Lily knows that this is the only way. Knowing it is different this time. Lily knows her victim. She wonders if she could help get Martha out of that evil man's influence.

She shows Terry the gun. Just to let him know that she had a way to protect herself and that she knew how to use it. Lily gives the card that she got from the officer. She looked at Terry and said, "Call him." "Tell him where I am." "I know where Martha is." "If we find her." "We found the sex trafficking ring."

"Which means my life could be in danger." "Make it sound urgent, because it is."

Sam looked at her and spoke. "Please be careful, Hony." "Sam's cousin means danger." "If he has Martha." "That means that she has his poison in her." "That will mean that she will need help." "Be careful, honey." "This could go the other way."

Lily looked at him and says to him. "Therefore, I need you to call this officer, NOW." "He will have to call for backup." "He knows what we talked about."

Terry looks at her. Knowing that she is right. Even thou he didn't want to admit it, she was right.

He knows that she could lose her life. Just to save a child, and it not his little girl. His heart sank with worry.

Not knowing if she would come back. Knowing that this is the reason. Why did she retire from being a military police investigator?

It would break her heart to see the children suffer. From the choices that adults would make.

This choice that Sam Cousin made for Martha. Is the one that she will pay for. Lily knows this. She has to save herself first. Then, they will work on the rest together.

Lily looks at Terry and speaks. "I need to go now." Terry gives her a kiss passionately. Just in case he doesn't see her again. Trying to be brave and let her go, but first they said a brief prayer. Then Lily turned around and walked away. Not knowing for sure if she would see him again.

Terry's heart raced. That it is coming to this. A big man. Putting his wife in danger. Knows that this is best. He is a man and doesn't like it one bit.

The only thing he could do was to do what she said. He picked up his cell phone. Dials the phone number. A man's voice is on the other end. Terry tells him who he is.

He talked earlier to Lily. Letting him know what is going on, and what Lily thought. "She suspected where the sex trafficking ring was," Terry says.

Terry, not knowing who the officer is. While the officer keeps him on the phone. Just so Terry could tell him where it was. The officer asks, "Where is your wife?"

Terry answered, she is in an abandoned car dealership. Terry asks the officer, "Please watch out for my wife". With the sound of a cracked voice. "She is my heart. I can't live without her."

The officer's voice was abrupt, then says, "What?". "I told her not to do anything." "Doesn't she listen?" Terry tells the officer, "My wife doesn't listen to anything to protect a child." "I don't know what to said." "She is a redhead."

"She believes in saving as many children that she can." "The innocent is what she needs to protect." "Her goal is to make the world a better place." "That is why she joined the Army as a Military Police Investigator." "She always thought that people should be able to live their lives freely."

"Just want you to know that she has a gun." "She will find Martha." Terry made sure that the officer knows that.

Lily is good at what she does. As the officer hangs up the phone, Terry follows. Terry turns around and sees Sam coming to. He knows that he keeps going in and out of the gray world.

Terry wants to be a good friend, but his mind is on his wife. He knows that she is walking right into danger to save his friend's daughter. Even if she would sacrifice. Her own life.

He knows that Sam couldn't do it. Everything is a big trail at this moment. Terry is questioning his Heavenly Father, but why?

Wondering why he is so hard on this family. Sam is out of it. Knowing this evil man takes Martha. Then his wife has to save her. Then Terry hears a whisper in his ear.

"Peace, be still". "Everything will work out, trust me". Terry looks around. Not knowing where it comes from. Thinking that it is Sam, but he is back to being in a gray world.

Terry couldn't believe what he was hearing. Again, a whisper in his ear. "Peace, be still." "Everything will work out." "Trust me."

He keeps looking around to see if someone is playing tricks on him. "Terry yelled out, this isn't funny." Not knowing who it could be.

He didn't know that his Heavenly Father was talking to him. He looks toward the heavens. Is this you? "Father, please tell me again."

"My wife is putting herself in danger for Martha". "Please bring them both home". A voice came back again for the third time.

Terry hears a soft voice. "Peace, be still". Everything will work out. "It is in my hands." Suddenly, love and peace came over him. *He knows that he needs to trust. He needs to have faith, and act on that faith.*

This is the hardest thing that he has ever done. Terry feels as if he put his wife on a chopping block. Just to know that Lily puts herself in danger. To save another innocent child. Just for this kind of action. She needs to do it. Wondering if she tries to save children because she didn't save her little girl.

He knows that she is out of sight, but he still gets out of the truck. Knowing that he can't even see her anymore. Deep down, he knows that everything will be good, for he was told. Peace be still.

Terry knows that he needs to wait for the officer to get there. Just to let him know where she went in.

Not knowing that this officer is a private investigator. Lily didn't know this either. This officer knows this area. Just like the back of his hand.

As the officer pulls up, Terry opens the truck door. Jump out of the truck. Just to meet him. Terry could tell that he was an undercover officer. He didn't have his uniform on; he was wearing casual clothes. As if he were a business owner, looking for trouble. The officer looked at him and said, "I want you to take your friend home."

"Then stay there until I call you." "This is not a place for you or your friend." Terry looks back at him. "What about my wife?" As the officer looks back at Terry. "I will have my team. Look out for your wife and for Martha. Go home."

Terry knows that he is right, but he didn't want to leave his wife there. Without him.

CHAPTER 14

EVIL HAS COME FOR ITS VICTIM

Meanwhile, Martha just stood there. Not knowing what to do. While her father's cousin comes towards her. With fear taking control, she has become frozen, as if she were a statue.

Sam's cousin grabs her arm. Leading her towards a place of doom. As he led her down to his hell, he remembered his daughter.

He killed her with his poison. Now that God took his daughter. He needs to take Sam's daughter. This must be done. Martha was frozen in fear, but still coherent. Knowing that she needs to get away from this evil man. She has seen his true colors. He will hurt her. Just to get even with her father.

She knows what her father always told her. Was to know her surroundings? She is trying to remember things and buildings around her.

Not knowing if she would ever see her father again. She knows that she has become his prey. She surrendered to his evil.

As she is walking, with her head downward. With the shame she felt of being prey to a lion. She didn't listen to her parents. Going to the city. Wondering would her father had kept these secrets? He was always honest with her mother.

While she thinks about all of this. She continues to notice all the original stuff that is around. Finally, they get to the place where he will leave her for a few moments.

She did not know what would happen next. Thumps of her heart say it all. She knows that she needs to get ready. Knowing this could be it. Wondering could she could meet her brother.

Her father's cousin will give her poison. She gets ready to meet her brother. Knowing that this could be it.

Martha will fight hard, but she knows the poison will win. She is only eleven, but knows what is going to happen. She has heard what her parents have said about him. What he has done. How he gives them poison.

As she continues to sit there, all these things come rushing into her mind. Now that there is nothing she can do. Wondering if she could hope to become free. Feeling such a fool to have fallen into such danger.

Remembered that Lily had told her to pray. When she is in a tight situation. To always remember him, he will help. She has nothing to lose. She bows her head and folds her hands. Asks her Heavenly Father for help. Knowing that she didn't know what to do. Knowing that he would answer her prayers. Not knowing how.

Her father's cousin shows back up. While Martha is saying her prayers. He looked at her while he said to her.

"I asked and prayed for my little girl to live." "He took her away." As he looked at her with angry eyes. While an evil laughter came.

She could see the evil in him. You will never see your parents again. I will sell you over and over. I will make so much money. Then, when I am done with you. I will sell you as a slave to someone else. With the words to remember. He continues looking at her and said, "What do you think of that?"

Martha just hung her head and continues praying. Feeling warmth on the back of her neck. Feeling the wrath of anger.

Just as if he weren't there. Knowing this is what her parents taught her to do. Not so much her mother, but her father did.

She would watch him. On her knees, asking his Heavenly Father. In humble prayer. She knows that her Heavenly Father will answer her prayer. He always did.

Sam's cousin is still standing there. Looking at her. Looking at her is in a jail cell, for her soul.

As she continues, he gives her an evil look. When she was done. She looks at him.

Through the tears. Hoping that he would give in to her and let her go home.

His eyes looked blackish, as if he had no soul. No feeling of any kind. It is just like someone or something. Sucked his soul out of him.

Martha didn't understand why he is like this. In so many ways. She is a child. Not understanding adult things. She thought she did. Martha is at the age that she thinks she knows everything. She knows nothing now. She knows that she is in big trouble.

While he shoves her into a metal cage. Seeing through the bar.

By now, she knows that he isn't going to let her go. Now that she knows this.

She looks around. No one is talking. It is like everyone is sleeping, as girls and boys came and went.

This is so freaky for Martha. Sam's cousin would just look at each girl that came and went. Knowing that each one brought something for him.

He looks at Martha as he gives her an evil grin. You will get your turn soon. Just wait. Soon, you will get what they have now. He continues to look at her. With the same evil grin. Knowing what the outcome, for her.

Knows that she couldn't leave. Even if she wanted to. His heart knows that this is wrong. His pleasure was in getting even with Sam. Is stronger than what is right.

His heart had hardened thew the years. No matter what, Sam and he. Had shared before.

He keeps thinking as he walks away. From the perspective of a child. Knowing that he comes from an evil way of thinking. His mind is telling him one thing, but his heart says another. While he keeps thinking of Martha.

His daughter comes to mind. He knows he would have gone to the end of the world for her. Just like Sam will. He knows that; it is too late for his daughter. He knows that it is too late for him as well.

The evil one has taken over him. He will do all of his bedding for him. Take as many innocent children with him, for he has become master of the apprentice.

He became an adversary of his God. The father of lies.

As he walks out, he looks back. Just to remind Martha. That she put herself in danger. That her father would risk everything for her. While he walks away.

She looks through the bars of steel, of the cage he put her in. Not quite understand everything that is going to happen to her. She knows that she did pray about it. Still not knowing.

Know that something should happen soon. Hoping and praying. Not knowing what.

As tears swell in her eyes, she remembers her parents. She knows that her father would care. Not knowing if her mother would.

She knows that her brother is more important than she is. To her mother. Martha sobbed. Not knowing for sure what is going to be in store for her.

Wondering if anyone could save her. From, the evil that will damage her.

Sitting in a cage for the first time. *Not knowing if she would become evil as well.* Martha will learn to become a servant for pleasure. Anyone who will pay for it. She will not get to choose.

While her wet droplets come. Falling from her eyes. Down onto her cheeks. She knows her life is gone. Her heart is breaking. This is the time she gets it. Being tricked by her father's cousin. She doesn't get the full scope of it. Just a fraction. She is a child. They will love her.

He has sworn that he would get even. She goes back in time. *Remembered, he had said this to her. The day of the funeral.*

Knowing that, by the way. She watched the girls come and go. Her turn will come soon. Being sold into the sexual trafficking world. She didn't even know it existed. Now she will live it.

As she began this journey, her body shook with fear. Backing up into the corner. Cold bars, reminding her where she is. *Her knowing that she cannot go any farther.*

Her days of freedom are gone. She is eleven-year-old. Some clients love young girls.

Not knowing what would happen next. She curls into a ball. While her body shakes. Like there is an earthquake within her.

While she continues, letting droplets come down her cheeks. She could hear.

A voice in the next cell, asking her. Are you going to be okay? Martha looks up. She could see a little girl. About eight or nine.

Now she knows she is in danger. As she looks at her, she asks her How long have you been here?"

She looked at her, and spoke. "I have been here for about two weeks." "That mean man brought me here." "He tells me this is where children go when their parents don't want them anymore." "They told me I need to be quiet here and not cry anymore." When I cry, it's because I'm hurt. I was told it was because I was bad. Then they give me a shot, and it goes away.

Martha looks at her and speaks. "Who told you to be quiet? "

The little girl crawls to the corner. While her eyes show. What is to come? It was time for her to be next. Knowing pain will come to her once more. Without making a sound. Hoping she could hide. As she shook, her fear showed.

Martha knows that she could be next. Her heart pounded through her chest. As they come closer to her. Wondering if she is the one. As they keep walking toward her, she knows that she is doomed. Hope is fading for her

She knows that if no one has found this little girl yet. Who will find her? Are they even looking? Martha could see this figure of a person; she could see it slow down.

She just knows it is coming for her. She knows that she needs to get ready for it. As she closes her eyes, praying silently for blessing from above.

Just to escape from the danger. As this person goes by, it passes her cell. They want the younger one.

Martha couldn't believe it. What would they do with her? How badly would they hurt her? Martha wants to save her, but how?

CHAPTER 15

FAITH IS WAVERING!

eanwhile, Jean is trying to do her best to stay calm. With her failing to stay out of the gray world. It wants to keep her there. In a world of doom. Its goal is to keep her there. It had become lonely for her.

Jean knows the truth, and who is behind her hopelessness. Knowing that she needs to get hold of the church. Just to let them know. They need to pray for Martha. That she is in danger. She knows that pray works. She has seen it time and time again.

Jean looks at Emmaline and speaks. "We need to call the church now."

"Could you call a few people", and I will call a few people." "We need to put Martha on the church pray list." We can't forget the temple pray list.

"This is what will keep her safe". Knowing all of this, prayer will save this family. Jean doesn't know everything that is going on with her daughter. But hoping that Heavenly Father would answer her prayer.

Knowing that the calls are done, they must wait.

Jean remembers reading her scriptures. It told her that when two or three. Have gathered in his name. That he would have answered. That he will be there.

Jean knows this. It has to happen to her. She just needs a little help. She knows that Emmaline is there to support her. Jean knows that this family needs more. She knows that; she needs to pray.

Her hopelessness is powerful. She can't do it on her own. She knows this. While she paced the floor again. Knowing that thing will be good by her Heavenly Father, just holding back a little.

Her faith is failing. She is the strong one with faith, but so many things are happening. That her faith is wavering.

Now she could fall into a gray world. Knowing that she needs to be stronger than ever for her daughter. Wanting to give in to the gray world.

While she questions herself. She wonders whether she can do this. If she could even help save her daughter.

She knows who has her. She hates him for what he is doing to her, as of now.

Her mind wondered. What could happen? She knows that he could be teaching her things. That no little girl her age should know.

Jean just knows how this feels, and she will try anything to keep her daughter safe. Her feeling of the dark comes to her. Lurked around to remind her of her childhood.

Her sticky red liquid boiled. What her father did to her. How could Sam's cousin do that to her daughter? Now doing it to their daughter.

There have been years of darkness, of this deed. As she keeps thinking about this, she wonders how someone could do this to another person.

While the gray world is patiently waiting for her to lose it. She isn't ready to go yet.

Thinking she needs to sit on the sofa. Start doing a breathing treatment on herself. Jean knows that her brain needs to slow down. It is racing too fast. Too much at one time. Knowing that she needs to stop pacing. One breath in, then out, that is one.

Knowing that this is the way. Without putting poison into her body. Jean looks at Emmaline and speaks. "Would you like to do this breathing treatment with me?" Emmaline looks back at her.

Just to get through this trail. Just one more trail. It seems to Emmaline that it is all Jean had. She turned to her and said to Jean. "This is a great idea." Jean looks back at her. "Sit here beside me."

Emmaline knows how to do it. *She used it on herself a few times. Almost every day, sometimes twice a day. She would also have her clients. Do this to calm them down.*

Knowing that she had a daughter. Is in danger. Jean knows that she has damaged herself. *Thinking she could not take back what she said.*

How is she going to concentrate on her breathing? *When her mind is on her daughter.*

Jean sits beside Emmaline. Wonders if it would work. *Even Emmaline wondered if Jean could do this.* She knows that Jean's mind is on her daughter. *Emmaline's mind is also on Martha. She feared for Martha. They both know how Sam Cousin is. She knows that Martha won't come back the same.*

Emmaline knows that this could break the family. This family is breaking, piece by piece. No one could have guessed. All the trails could break this family up. This family has been through so much. Losing a baby boy before their son. Having a stillborn. Then their son was hit by a car and passing.

While sitting on the sofa. Trying to do a breathing treatment with Jean. It wasn't working for her. Her mind is in another place. Trying to support her friend, but just can't seem to keep her mind on track.

Every once in a while. She would look at Jean beside her.

Jean is trying her best to keep her mind in the right place. She is having a hard time as well. She just couldn't keep her mind on task either.

Her daughter is the theme of her thoughts. She lost count of the breaths she had taken. Jean just couldn't do it anymore. Her frustration is too much. She keeps trying to count her breaths.

Knowing the gray world is coming for her again. She knows it's coming. Sooner than she wants.

She knows that prayer works. She has tried it already. What is she to do? She didn't want to take her medication. Jean feels like she has failed herself. She is trying not to depend on her drugs. Just to calm her down. She didn't like what it did to her. It puts her in another world. At this moment, she wants to be on this one.

She wants to be on this earth when they find Martha. With the sound of a sigh. As it became frustration, knowing that she had had enough of wasting her time. This breathing treatment wasn't working this time.

Jean looks towards Emmaline. Just to see if she is doing the breathing treatment. She could see that Emmaline was having a hard time as well. Not knowing what to do. She stops. Hoping that this would end soon.

Not caring for anything else. It is the time for her to get better, for her family.

She looks at Emmaline. Knowing there must be a way for her. To get some kind of help.

Jean tells "her I can't do this anymore." "There has to be a way for me to function." "Without drugs." "I need to be in this world." "I need to be that mother to my daughter. "She needs a mother who will love her." "I have made so many mistakes." "She needs to have it shown to her." "I need to show her."

"I have been here, but yet I'm not." "Why did it take this long?" "Just to get me to see this."

Emmaline didn't know what to says. She continues to look at Jean. tells her, "I know from experience." "This is a hard thing to handle." "It's not fair." "Life can give us challenges, Jean." While she looks at her, she continues. Telling her she needs to keep going. "You know, your daughter really needs you."

Jean looks up at her. Looking at her eyes. She could see that she knows how. She felt.

Emmaline has the same problem. She does, but she has found out how to deal with it. Jean knows that Emmeline has the same problem. A lighter case. She continues looking as she asks Emmaline for help. "How do I do this? "What is your advice? "

Emmaline's heart broke for her. She knows what it is like to feel hopelessness.

She knows that could be a miss. Just to find the right medicine. It could be months. With each person being different.

Right at this moment. They need to get Martha back first.

Then work on Jean's medication. She knows that it wouldn't do any good. To change it now.

Changing her medication could put her in a deeper, hopelessness gray world.

Then she is now. She knows that she might have to use drugs. Just to calm her down. Sam had to use them on her before. A few times.

While Emmaline is wondering about her.

Jean wonders about herself. How is she going to do this?

Then she began thinking about Martha again. *What is happening to her? Is she going to be good? How much damage will happen to her? Wondering what kind of damage. There will be. Knowing that she will come back.*

She knows this from her prayers. Her silent prayers. She knows that she has peace. In her heart.

She doesn't know how to react to it. Emmaline could tell that there was something different on Jean's mind.

Something besides what she has been through.

As she looks back at Jean, she wonders if she is going to get through this with her. She just knows that once this trial is done. She will learn something from this.

Wondering, however, if this trail would have to be done again.

Martha at this time is in danger.

Emmaline begins a silent prayer. Knowing that her Heavenly Father is listening to her. He is here. She knows this. She just needs to be reminded. In her mind and in her heart. Just to know that her Heavenly Father has everything in control. She knows that her Heavenly Father. Will never leaves.

She can't deny it. She has an overwhelming feeling of peace. *Emmaline first thought, is what about Jean?*

If only she could give her this feeling. Just maybe Jean could be at peace also

But little did Emmaline know that Jean was doing her own prayers. For the first time in Jean's life, she was at peace as well.

Knowing that her Heavenly Father had already told her what would happen. She has complete faith in him at this moment. Knowing the dream that she had. She knows this wasn't just a dream. It was a vision.

A prophetic from her Heavenly Father. The warning that is coming true now.

She knows that if she doesn't change some things. That this could go the wrong way. Her daughter could lose. This warning is to let her know that she needs to change.

She needs to teach her daughter that there is hope in Heavenly Father. No matter what it is.

This is going to strengthen her faith. She knows this. She has been on her knees more this week. More than she ever has before.

Her humility has taken her to her final place. On her knees, before her Heavenly Father. She remembers what her Heavenly Father would tell her. He will heal her broken heart. She remembers a Bible verse, say that Psalm 147:3(He heals the broken in heart, and bidet up their wounds). She remembers this from her childhood. Her Sunday school teacher taught her this.

Even thou her father told her different. It took her years. Just to think that she could be the person her Heavenly Father would want. Why would he want her? She felt as if she were worth nothing. Knowing she knows that Jesus Christ died for her. Jean, for the first time. She knows that she is worth everything to him. He is working for her. Peace be with her now. The thought is still with her. What about her daughter?

CHAPTER 16

WALKING INTO DANGER!

Lily is trying to be quiet and not to be noticed.

She slinks across the ground. Trying to look as if she belongs there. Knowing that she gets caught. She and Martha would be in danger.

Could even lose their lives or be taken to where no one would ever find them. She prayed for guidance. Knowing that it would take his wisdom on her. To save them both, and maybe save others...

Her heart thumped through her chest. Knowing that at any moment they would see her. She notices a big man walking by while she is bending down. Behind a mental crate. Hoping that he didn't see her. Holding her breath, so that no sound would come out. *Praying in her mind as well. Listening to footsteps going by.*

Lily didn't know what shape Martha would be in. She knew that if she could reach her in time. Martha would be safe. Maybe even other girls.

While the footsteps faded. Her throat is in her stomach. It wants to bring up its lunch. Lily knows that the cost looks as if it is ready. Not knowing for sure. She knows that she has to take a risk. As she looks, she crawls down. She knows that the mental crates would hide her.

Knowing that she is still carrying. Lily knows that if she is to use it. It could give her away.

She knows how these guys think. She would have to become one of them. As she got closer to the doors, she saw a crowd of men and women.

They are here to buy the girl, so Lily thought. While her blood boiled. She knows that she needs to be in control of her feelings.

She has been in this situation in Afghanistan. Lily gets her man. She knows that Sam's cousin is involved in this one. He knows what she looks like, and she knows he is here. As she follows the crowd, hoping she doesn't run into Sam's cousin. Walking through the crowd. In and out. The crowd moved toward a room. She knows what will happen soon. As they move closer, she moves in the opposite direction.

Knowing that she needs to act as if she knows where she is going. She keeps walking, watching as she goes. Knowing that she needs to find Martha now.

Her fear now is that Martha will sell quietly. Then she may never be seen again. As she is walking, she sees men walking around. No one seems to notice her. It is as if no one could see her. She knows that these men went through these double doors.

That seems strange to her. Why did they do this? There is something in there. There has to be, but what? She could see. How these people are all dressed in white.

Her mind was that of an investigator. Lily needs a disguise, and she just found one. She knows that this is her way in. Lily looks upward to tell her Heavenly Father, in her mind, thanks.

This wisdom came from him, and she knows it. Not knowing what might happen next. She had the faith to move forward. Not knowing what will happen? Just knowing to move forward is what she needs to do. As she walks through the door.

She notices a little girl. She couldn't be any older than eight.

Lily knows what it looks like. These people, that are dressed in white. Have drugged her. Knowing that they had to know why they were doing this. To this beautiful child. Just to prep her for a client.

Lily wanted to scream, and she did. In her mind. She knows that it wouldn't do anyone any good.

If she exposed herself. She would be in danger.

Then what would happen to Martha? For she could save Martha, and also others. She knows that if she doesn't do this, who will?

The government trained her. Just for jobs like this. She would do the dirty work.

She hated to do this. These indecent faces. As she keeps thinking to self, she sees another set of white doors.

She knows that she needs to get there. Just to see what is so important. What would be on the other side? She knows it is going to be worse. For there could be younger, just to satisfy. A sick person.

The man brought his evil deeds here. As she thinks more to herself, she knows she needs to get in there now.

How many innocent lives are here?

She knows why she got out of this line of work. It was on its way to destroying her. She saw too many of her friends. Kill themselves, overseeing too much damage. In young lives, as small as infants. Some weeks to months old.

Some predators don't care how old they are.

Lily knows the damage that people can cause. She tries to keep trying. Trying not to draw attention to herself. Knowing with each step. They could find her.

Her heart thump. She could hear the beat of a tune in her mind. Not realizing that Sam's cousin is close to her, just a few steps away. She had a feeling that she needed to move slowly to the side. Something told her to be wary. To move towards the doors quietly. This feeling of the dome. Was having her. Wanting to bring her nerves to it end. Lily sees an opening to move. She moves. Asking her Heavenly Father. To help her make it through the white doors. Knowing she would find destruction. Lily's primary goal at this moment is to find Martha. In the back of her mind. Hoping to save all the children.

Her heart is full of sorrow at knowing those people. Have let themselves become so evil.

She looks ahead. Just a few more inches to go. Knowing that someone could stop her at any moment. While she keeps praying. Knowing that he is the only one that will keep her safe.

She inches closer to the doors. Trying to be ready to see horror. She gets to the door. Closed her eyes. Takes a deep breath. Just to get ready to look horror in the face. Knowing that her heart will be breaking. Lily doesn't understand why. As Lily opened her eyes.

She looks at all the children. There are hundreds of children. Trapped in cages. Most of them were drugged. Not knowing where they are. Not knowing that their families are looking for them.

Her heart breaks as she looks around. Someone needs to save them, but who? She knows that she needs to keep her pose.

While inside, she is screaming, while she keeps her tears back. She knows that her Heavenly Father is in control, but at this moment.

She is human and wants justice for the innocent. People who do this should be killed. While she says this in her brain.

Lily knows where this evil is coming from. She knows the father of lies. Is there a here for their souls? Including the innocent.

Martha is one of them.

She thinks back to the time when she lost her little girl. She knows that she would have done anything to save her. Martha is the girl she would want. She has a connection to her.

She looks around for her. All the cages. She is so lost wondering which one. Roles and the role of cages. She could see these girls and boys caged like animals. The law forgot them.

She continues to look. Knowing she is getting angrier by the moment. Seeing babies, being treated like trash. She knows that when they are done. They will die. In so many ways.

Lily kept trying to hold her pose. It is coming to the top. Her heartbreak is showing. She knows that she needs to swallow the lump of sorrow.

Lily knows that she needs to stop and breathe. She leans up against one cage. Lily looks down at the floor as she looks up. She notices a baby, only a year old. Lily gets wet eyes. That baby looked as if it were dead. She will remember this one. It could have been her little girl.

"How can man be so evil?"

CHAPTER 17

WAITING FOR GOOD NEWS!

eanwhile, Terry is waiting for the Undercover Cop. Wondering if his wife is close to Martha yet. He knows that she wouldn't stop. Until she finds her.

He had faith that she would come back. Lily is good at what she does.

His heart is beating so hard. It just might beat through his chest. Having faith is harder for him. He knows that it is easier for Lily.

All he wants at this moment is to see her. His wife walked towards him with Martha, but faith doesn't work that way. It will test him. He wonders if his Heavenly Father is listening to him. He keeps praying. Hoping that his prayers get answered. His wife is his world. If something happens to her. His life will end.

He knows that she has done this before, but anything could happen to her. He knows she is carrying. It could be good for her or bad. He knows that she knows how to use a gun.

As he keeps looking out the window, Sam wakes up. Not knowing where he is. He looked at Terry and asks him, "What happened?" "Is Martha okay? Terry looked at him and said, don't you remember anything that happened?" "Sam said "no". "I don't". He continues to look at Terry. With a look of confusion.

Not to remember the activity of the day. Remembered his son's funeral. Then his heart sank.

He wanted to go back to the gray world of forgetfulness. To live in bliss. Life had other plans for him. He is to live his heat ace.

Terry keeps trying to talk to Sam, but his mind is on his wife. He is trying to be a good friend, but he can't.

He wants to run and find her. To keep her safe. He knows that if he is to run in there. Before Lily could save Martha. He could be gone. Terry knows this!

So, he talks to Sam. He knows that Sam needs to stay awake. Sam has been out of it too much. He needs to be there for his daughter.

Besides, Terry is still waiting for the Undercover Cop for an update. He needs to save her, so Terry thinks. As he keeps talking to Sam, he keeps looking out the back window. Wondering when he will show up. Lily could be dead by then.

Terry's faith is wavering. He is praying for a miracle. At this moment, it is being tested. Terry wondered if he is going to pass. This is a test. Terry keeps talking, trying his best.

Not to let Sam know what is happening. With Lily or Martha. He didn't want to let Sam know. This is his cousin, who took Martha. This is so heartbreaking for Sam. He is going to go against family. To protect the family. His Daughter.

He knows at this moment. It is so close for him to run in there. Just to see if she is alive. Remembering why Lily went in there.

What could they be doing to Martha?

Sam looks at him. He could tell from the look on his face. Something's wrong, really wrong. For Sam didn't know what had happened and what was happening right now. Why is his friend so troubled about an old empty automobile shop?

Every once in a while, he could see a teen shuffling in and out of doors. Walking around, but not knowing why? Not knowing that his daughter is in there. That his cousin trapped her. In a dark, evil cave, never to be realized again. At this moment.

Sam is doing all that he can. His strength is coming back slowly. Everything is a haze to him. He puts the pieces together.

He did not know that his cousin was going to get back today. Sam doesn't know what is going to happen.

But he remembers. Sam continues talking to Terry. He looks across toward the empty car lot. He thinks he sees his cousin. Thinking to himself. How odd that would be. Why would he be there? It wouldn't be his kind of place.

He looks at Terry with an odd look. Asking him why we are here? Not knowing that Terry is waiting for someone. He is still mumbling a little. Still having a problem with his speech. But understanding a little more of what has happened. He knows that the only way to get answers is to ask questions. Is to ask?

He looked at Terry and said to him. "What is happening." "Why are we here, and not home?" "I should be with my wife and daughter." "Grieving over Steven."

Terry tries his best not to look at him directly. Trying to keep his pose. Not to tell him everything at once. It will be too much for him. Overloaded his brain. It could even put them in danger.

He doesn't even know. How much danger Martha is in? Terry knows that if he had told him about Martha at that moment. He could get them all killed.

Terry knows that he needs to tell him, but not now. He tells him. He needs to wait for someone. Not letting him know who.

Sam did not know why? They would wait there. Sam continues to ask where Martha and Jean are. He looks at Sam.

Tells Sam that Jean is with Emmaline and Martha is with Lily. Terry knows that it is a matter of time. Before he figures it out.

Terry hates himself. He knows that Sam is going to be so angry at him for not telling him.

What is happening to his daughter? Terry just wants this to turn out well for Sam's family. He knows they have a long road ahead of them.

He knows that something happens. To Martha, Sam will never recover. They all need each other. Just to survive.

Sam's cousin can cause so much damage.

How can this happen? Terry doesn't understand how a man of God is. Could fall so hard from grace. In such a short time. Just ten years ago. He was on a mission.

Terry knows one thing. Martha will pay for being so rebellious. This will be one thing she will remember forever.

Terry prays under his breath. Lily is hoping. Lily will get to Martha in time. While he is praying.

Sam is still trying to remember. The events of the day. Is still blurry. He remembers a brawl with his cousin. It was over for Martha.

He looks at Terry. "Is Martha safe?" His eyes were full of fear. Sam's deepest fear was that his cousin got ahold of her.

He would fill her full of his poison. Terry knows that he couldn't lie to him anymore. He looks at him, knowing that he has to tell him the truth.

Terry wishes that this day were done. He would rather be anywhere else. Sam is his best friend. Like a brother. How is he going to tell him? Martha would as a sex slave? Casting a poison that would never satisfy. Until she takes.

How could he tell him? Terry continues, looking at him. He swallows' a lump in his throat. Hoping that could pass him by.

Terry tells him what is going on. About his cousin having Martha. How Lily is in trying to save her. That it is happening at this old car dealership.

While the undercover cop drives up next to the truck. He opens the car door. Getting out of the car. Shutting the door. Coming around to the driver's door.

Terry gets out. Undercover cop talks to Terry. Sam knows by now. Something is very wrong. Martha is in danger. He has to save her. Even if he dies by saving her.

Now is the time to find out. He sees more undercover cops. Gathering together in a group. He could see pistols hanging from their belts.

Now he knows something is desperately wrong. He knows that it had to do with his cousin.

He knows down in the pit of his stomach. Martha is in danger. Now he knows it is time to get on his knees. He knows there is nothing else that can be done.

His hope has to lie with his father. Knowing he feels so helpless. He can't help anyone. He feels better, but weak.

Still wanting to know what the undercover cops are doing. He opens the truck door. Steps out. Feeling as if he is going to go to the gray world.

Terry, seeing him, comes toward him. He walks over to meet him. By the truck door, while the undercover cop followed him.

Undercover cop reaches out to shake Sam's hand. Sam reaches out to shake. Sam asks, what is going on? Undercover cop says, we are here to break up a sex trafficking ring." "We believe that your daughter is in there."

"There is an insider in there." "We are in touch with them." "Just as soon as they give us the go head."

Sam couldn't says anything. His Daughter. What is going to happen? All of this is coming to a head. He knows that his cousin is involved in this.

He said that he would get even with him. Sam can't let him win. Sam knows where to go. On his knees. He knows that Heavenly Father. Will take care of it. It will take faith and hope. Sam knows that the Heavenly Father will fight for him and his daughter.

Terry continues looking at Sam. He just knows? Sam could pass to the gray world again. Sam's face is saying it all. At this moment. He is still weak.

Terry wondered what Sam would do next. Terry has known Sam all his life.

He didn't know what Sam would do. Terry knows that Sam has never been in this situation before. Terry could always able to read Sam's mind, but he couldn't this time.

He knows that Sam, being a father, would want to fight. All Sam can do is watch. With a heart-ace. His heart is being ripped out of his chest. Watching his friend's heartache is too much.

There isn't anything more heart- breaking to watch. He knows there is nothing he can do.

For the first time. Sam can't protect his family. His family members will damage his daughter.

This is going to hurt his family for a lifetime. It has become a bad T.V. show. Only this is really happening. Terry watches Sam. Just to be sure. Sam stays put.

He knows that Sam will run towards danger to save his little girl.

While Terry and Sam talk to the undercover cop. Sam looks across to the car dealership. Watching the activity. It looks as if there is a business. Nothing to suspect a sex ring.

Sam is weak, and he knows this. He knows that he needs to be there for his daughter.

He needed to be stronger. Then he is now. He knows where he could get it. As his mind wanders, he looks towards the sky. The car dealership. The more he looked, the more fear set in.

Faith is what he needs at this moment. He knows this, but he is human. Sam is the one who has a strong faith, but not now. It is wavering. He is being tested. He is wondering whether he will pass.

As Terry and he continued to talk with the undercover cop, he thought that he needed to do all he could to bring Martha back. That would include him to go in.

He knows that it could fail, but he has to try. He didn't know that Lily was already in there.

Terry didn't tell him yet. He knows that something is going on with Terry, but he doesn't know what.

Sam is observing Terry. Knowing that something is wrong. He knows that Terry isn't telling him everything. While they both continue to talk to the undercover cop. Sam did not quite understand everything going on. Something wasn't right.

Sam looks at Terry knowing something is off. Terry is talking to himself. Deep down, he is hiding something.

When Sam was unconscious. He could still hear him, but he didn't know where Lily was.

He thought he had heard her at one time. But wasn't sure. Sam knows by talking to the undercover cop. Martha is in danger.

Deep down within him. He knows that his cousin is a big part of this. Knowing he is family, he doesn't care who he hurts. Even if it is blood. He has to see for himself. He knows he needs to watch his back. His cousin would hurt him or even kill him. He knows about the poison. His cousin would give. His own poison to any soul. That would take it. Sam keeps thinking to himself.

He has to get in there to save his daughter. He knows that Terry would stop him if he just knew what he is thinking.

Terry was so worried about Lily he didn't even notice. What could Sam be up to? He knows that for now? Sam is too weak to do anything unexpected, or so he thought. He knows that Sam would be where he had put him.

With the door open. Sitting on the truck seat. Little did he know what Sam was planning. Sam wants his cousin to pay for what he is doing. He knows that his cousin has become evil. He is taking the innocence of a child. It is time for him to be stopped, even if he is dead. He knows that it would be best for one person to die. Then, for him to destroy more innocent lives. He knew that he believed in the death penalty. He also believed in living.

Sam knows that Terry had a gun in the glove-box. He also knows that he will need it for safety.

If Terry knew what he was about to do. He would stop him.

Knowing that the undercover cop. Would have him watched, so he couldn't botch the bust of the sex ring.

Sam knows there needs to be a distraction. Then he could sneak off. Without being noticed. He looks around. Wondering what could be that distraction.

Terry moved towards him. Sam takes a deep breath. Knowing his heart could beat through his chest. Hoping Terry doesn't see him with the gun. Knowing this isn't a good sign. He needs Terry to be distracted.

At that moment, the undercover cop. Waved for Terry to come over. To the other side of his car. Terry nods his head and raises his hand. Gets ready to head over. Wondering what he needs to know.

CHAPTER 18

HEADING INTO DANGER!

Sam knows that this is the moment to go. Towards an empty car shop. Where danger could wait for him. Sam didn't think about the danger. He is going to save his daughter. From his cousin's poison, could wait for her. He had been a hero before, having saved a few men before. In a war.

Knowing that it could be the last time. To see Martha. Hoping that his legs would keep him going. That his brain would be alert. Like it was.

When he was in the Army. Knowing to be on guard. He learned this when he did a tour of Afghanistan. His life was in danger more than once. He might have to use Terry's piece.

He leaped toward the door. This place of doom, where his daughter is. He knows that he might not even recognize her. If his cousin had his way. She could be full of his poison. Not knowing where she is.

He wondered if she could be almost dead or sold for a profit. They would take her out of the country. Even into a foreign land. He remembers the flashback. When he was in the Army, but this isn't at this moment.

He needs to get back to the task at hand. This is about his daughter. Not his flashbacks. He is wondering why he is thinking about his past?

He knows that he needs to watch out for Terry. Just hoping he doesn't notice. Sam walked slowly around Terry. While Terry is talking to the undercover cop. As Sam holds his breath, he tiptoes. Around him.

Trying not to pass out. Knowing that he goes too fast. He could head toward the gray world. He needs to stop and take a breath. As he leans against an old building, he slides down. While he is trying to take slow breaths. Knowing he is heading toward grayness. Knowing that anyone could find him. Hoping that no one has seen him. He just wants to save his little girl.

How is he going to do this? Rational thinking isn't in his plans. While he continues to talk to himself. *His blood is boiling within him. Wondering why he couldn't get it together. Feeling like a failure because he is so weak. How could one small fall? Take everything out of him.*

Sam knows that he needs to press forward. He didn't want Terry to know that he was gone. Terry would go after him. To stop him. Sam thinks he did not have to be on this mission. *No one could do it like he could. This is a mission that is top priority. It is worth more than he is. This thing of red sticky liquid. It became water. It ended his army career.*

He will not let it end his daughter. He will find her. Even if he dies from it. He will save her.

Sam stands up. Shakes his head and gets ready. He heads toward the car dealership. Knowing that he is going right into danger. Knowing that he might not come back. Not knowing that Lily is already in there trying to save her.

He knows that his Heavenly Father is watching over him as he is praying under his breath. Felling the peace as he goes. Knowing that he will get strength from him. Sam could feel a power of strength as he was trying not to be noticed. The closer he gets. His heart beat to the tune of danger. Sam knows the closer he is. He could put him and Martha in so much danger. As Sam gets closer.

Terry looked over in his direction. Not realizing at first. That it could be his friend. Terry keeps watching.

Knowing that more undercover cops. Will show up soon. Wondering when the undercover cops would arrive. Could they even save his wife? Could they even be able to stop the sex trafficking ring? Terry just wishes this whole thing were done. He doesn't like it. When his wife. Put her life in a life-and-death situation.

Terry doesn't enjoy waiting. He paces back and forth. While he becomes more and more frustrated. Asking when they are going to go in.

Not realizing that there is already an undercover cop in there. Let them know what is going on. The cop is representing as a buyer. When it goes down. They will go in. Then hell will break out. Little did they know that Sam was already in there. He is out for justice. Ready to take a life.

CHAPTER 19

WALKING TOWARDS DANGER!

alking through a dark hall. Passing rooms. Being silent, sneaking past. Men who looked as if they were going to buy children.

Sam walks through the double doors. He thought that he had seen everything evil before. However, he didn't. This is one thing he will not forget easily. He has had nightmares before.

This one is worse, for children are everywhere. While Sam keeps walking. He sees these white metal doors. Trying not to look at the people dressed in white. They have the look, as if they were Doctors.

He knows that he needs to hasten. Just to make sure he doesn't draw attention to himself. He knows that his cousin is somewhere. He needs to watch out for him. While he is trying to walk around quietly.

He ends up with the buyers. He knows that he is in a critical situation. This is bad, and he knows it. The only thing he can do is go along with it.

He knows that he has his piece, but it will only hurt or kill one. Sam isn't playing around. Knowing that if he has to use it, he will. He is there for one thing, and that is his daughter.

He knows that he needs to hang out in the back. Moving towards the back slowly. Where the light isn't that good. It is harder to see anything back there. He knows that they couldn't see him.

As everyone was gathering, he heard a familiar voice. Sam tries his best to get closer, for it rings in his ears. He knows who it is. He knows without a doubt who it is. His heart breaks.

He knows who his cousin serves. Knowing that he needs to move. Knows that if his cousin would see him. It would be over.

Sam knows that he needs to get out of there NOW. He crept toward the door. The double white doors are for the buyer. Are getting ready to move through them. Thinking he saw Lily slip out, but was not sure.

Sam knows that this is the time for him to get out of there. Just as soon as he can. He knows that his cousin would spot him. Then it would be over. All the work that he did. Would be done. He needs to finish this mission. It is more important than any other. While they walk through the door.

Sam spots a way to move to the right. Without anyone knowing, he left.

Sam did not know what he would run into. Hoping that he could. Move forward toward his daughter. While he turns around the corner. He runs into a tall man.

With bulging muscles. This could crush a small man and rip him in two parts. Knowing that this man could kill him in one hit. He knows that he has to play along with him.

Sam looked at him and said, "I am lost". Sam tried not to give himself away. Trying to keep himself calm. His heart beat so hard.

You could see it beating through his chest, so he thought. As the man looks at him, Sam looks around. Hoping to throw this man off suspicion.

Sam knows that this man is dangerous. He could botch the mission. He acted as if Sam was there to buy girls and boy, for a small sex ring. As he looks at Sam, he tells him.

That he could take him to the room. Where do they make the bedding? Sam knows that this isn't good. As he follows this man, he is praying all the way. Hoping that his cousin doesn't see him. Knowing that he's doomed. His cousin will notice him.

If the Heavenly Father doesn't intervene. Martha and his life will be gone. Also, anybody else who is in the way.

As they get closer to the betting room. Sam's heart beat faster. His body tries its best to go gray. His stomach knows what he ate earlier, as he tries to keep it down. The lump in his throat is stuck. While he is trying so hard. To swallow it down. Just to act as if he is there to buy sex slaves.

Knowing that his daughter could be one of them. This is making him sick with anger. Knowing that they have come to a place of evil. To the room that will destroy souls. The man walked into the room to introduce Sam. Not knowing his name. He looks at Sam and asks for a name.

Sam couldn't think of a name, so he looked at him. Hoping that his cousin didn't notice him. Just call me Baldy. Sam's cousin looks at him.

It is as if he is going to stare a hole through him. Sam is putting his hand on his piece. Just in case all hell broke loose. His cousin looked at him hard for a bit. It is as if he knows who Sam is. Then again, maybe not.

CHAPTER 20

QUESTIONING OF WHY?

Meanwhile, back with Jean and Emmaline. Things are calming down. Emmaline fixes some food for Jean, so she could take her medicine.

While Jean continues pacing back and forth. Chewing her nails. Hoping that all of this will end soon. Knowing that this is going to take everything from her.

Why did Martha do this? Doesn't she know that this isn't about her?

As she keeps walking, she knows her Heavenly Father. Has his own plan. *Why would Martha do this? Was it to get even with her?*

With a memory going back a few days.

When Martha and her son. Would play in the backyard, or fight. She knows that her family will not be the same. Jean knows that all of this isn't Martha's fault. Martha is only eleven years old. Jean understands that Martha is a child. She doesn't understand at this moment that Martha needs her mother.

Her mother's love, and her understanding. Jean blamed Martha for her son's death and now regrets it.

Martha didn't watch him. All the anger that Jean has inside of her. Suddenly, a voice beside her. Whispering in her ear. You know this isn't true. It isn't anyone's fault. It is hopeless to blame one another.

I have this. Your son is safe. He has always been mine. I just shared him with you.

Jean realizes where this is coming from. She finally got it. What she is doing. It took a whisper in her ear to get to reality. Not knowing why, she would blame a child.

Jean is at peace once more, knowing that this came from above.

Emmaline finished in the kitchen. With the cooking. Just to make sure that Jean had something to eat. She needs to take her medication.

She didn't want her to go to the gray world. Once she is there. She could go deep into the gray world. Maybe she won't come back at all.

As she comes out of the kitchen, with food for Jean. She notices that, Jean. Stop passing the floor by the sofa. She seems at peace. Emmaline knows that this could last for a bit. Not for long.

Jean needs to take her medication to sleep. She knows that all of this could go badly for her.

She just buried her son. Now, her daughter is in danger. Maybe even gone as well. She knows that deep down. Jean is blaming herself.

Emmaline knows Jean's father. Has told that the reason that her son is gone. Is because she is a bad girl. He has always told her.

He may do whatever he wants to do. With her or her children. He is the patriarch of the family. Since her brother is dead. She is the only one left. That it is his right. This is the reason she wouldn't bring her daughter to him. He would do the same to her.

Emmaline knows that this is the reason. Jean would have a problem with her depression.

Emmaline walks over to the sofa; she hands the food over. She looks into Jean's eyes. Telling her that everything will turn out good.

While Jean bows her head. To remind Emmaline to thank Heavenly Father for the food. Jean prayed. Reminding her Father in heaven of her pain.

She has the heart-ace. She also has a peace. Her Heavenly Father has given a revelation. Jean knows. She can't deny it. He has told her more than twice.

She knows that she needs to eat something. Before she took her medication. Her body is letting her know. She needs to rest. It is about to give in. She looked at Emmaline and spoke. "If I fall asleep, and you know I will." "If we get a phone call." "Wake me, please." "I want to know what is happening." "Please don't leave without me." "This is my precious daughter."

Emmaline looks at Jean for a few seconds. Not knowing what to say. She had never heard her call Martha her precious daughter before.

Jean lets Emmaline know that she loves her daughter. Just don't know how to show it.

The only love that Jean got was the wrong love. It damaged her in so many ways. She wants Emmaline to promise.

Emmaline just looked at her. Just to let her know. She would do anything for her friend. As they both ate, they had an understanding.

Emmaline looks at Jean and tells her. This can go bad. Jean looks back at Emmaline and said, "I want to see her." "Even if they found her body, without her spirit." "I want to see her."

Emmaline looks back into her eyes. Just to let her know that she is there for her. Jean, for the first time, really understood. That she is at fault in her treatment of Martha.

She blamed her daughter for her brother's death. Who does that? Give the blame to a little girl who is hurting herself.

She becomes angry with herself. Knowing what she has put on her daughter. She failed her.

Her grayness is setting in on her again. While Jean continues to eat her food. She felt sick to her stomach. Knowing what kind of mother she is.

She looks at Emmaline. Shakes her head. Trying to let Emmaline know. That the grayness is back.

Wondering if the past few days could disappear. Could she have a do-over?

Her feeling of the gray world is coming for her. Emmaline knows that Jean needs her medication now.

Emmaline walks quickly over to the kitchen. Got her bottle of medication. Knowing that she needs it now.

Emmaline knows this trail. Could destroy this family.

She opens the bottle and gets the medication that is required, knowing that she needs it now. Emmaline hands it over to Jean.

Looks at her and tells her to take it now. Jean knows that this will help her, but hates what it does to her.

Jean put it in her mouth. Then began eating the rest of her food. Know that she will sleep soon.

Not quite thinking about Martha. At this moment. Her taking her medication. She won't know what will happen to her daughter until she wakes up. Jean looks at Emmaline and said, "I know that I need to head to my bed."

Jean sets her plate on the end table. Stands up and heads towards the stairs. Goes up one by one. Knowing that the medication will do its job soon. She knows that she will be out in the dream world once more.

Jean hated being this way. The medication would always make lose control of herself. She doesn't have control over anything.

While she is walking, she is thinking about these things. Wondering if this is her fault. As she gets into her bed, knowing that soon she is in dreamland. Not being in reality at a bad time.

As Jean gets into her bed, wondering if her daughter will be safe. She lay down on her pillow and closed her eyes. Knowing that the medication is working.

Knowing who is behind all of this. The one that got her daughter.

The medication has worked for her. She heads to dreamland. She dreams of evil.

Dreaming of a fog of darkness. Not knowing where to find her family. A dark shadow was cast over her. Trying to capture her. Just to let her know that she has a family. Would be in his control. This evil fog of darkness. Is out to destroy everything good about this family.

There is nothing she can do in her dreams. She just has to watch.

CHAPTER 21

LOOKING AT EVIL!

Meanwhile, Lily forces herself to move on. While her heart breaks for those babes. Knowing the only thing to do is to move forward. She needs to find Martha. As she passed cage by cage. Kids being caged as if they were trash. As she passed each cage, she dripped red sticky liquid. Boiled within her.

Lily wants these people to pay for what they have done. Where is the justice? She knows that she needs to put her attention somewhere. On her task. She needs to find Martha now.

This is becoming more dangerous, just like it was in Afghanistan.

Lily knows. That if she is to be caught, it will be by the white coats. If they found her, it would be over.

She knows that she needs to find a way. To look like she belongs. How would that happen? She needs to look like a worker. How is that going to happen? Looking around her, surrounding. Seeing people in white coats. With a clue that came to her brain.

She would have to look like a doctor. She needs a white coat, but where? At all costs, she needs to blend in. She is looking for a room.

While she keeps praying for Martha. To be alive. That she could get to her. Before any harm comes to her. Knowing that anything could happen. Also, knowing that miracles can happen as well. She has seen them.

Lily knows that she has to leave it. In Heavenly Father's hands and move on. Martha is safe in his hands. She needs to find that room. While she keeps hoping for it to be soon. Knowing this is the best thing to do.

There is a strong feeling to do this. This strong feeling has saved her more than once. Lily knows that she needs to go to the other side. Where she is. She heads back. The same places. She came before. Praying as she goes not to be seen. Asking her Heavenly Father as she goes by these innocent children. Praying to her Heavenly Father. That she doesn't let a broken heart stop her.

So many children need to be saved. As she walks by, she prays for justice. They are doing evil. She keeps walking. Wondering if she is ever going to get to the right room. To get a white coat. Just to fit in and not get noticed. Just to walk by.

Her job is to save Martha. As she walks by each cage, her heart breaks. Just to know. That she has to walk by and do nothing. Just to do her job. Just to save Martha.

Lily finally sees a door to a big room. She goes in as if she walks in there. No one notices her. Her heart is letting her know that it is there. She can feel every thump that it makes. The lump in her throat is stuck. It is making itself known. Lily is trying to make sure. She doesn't give herself away. She sees a white coat. Grabs it and puts it on really quick.

Not wanting to hear that voice. That she doesn't want to see. Hopping to avoid. He is right behind her. He didn't know that Lily was right there. Lily tries so hard to swallow the lump. That is there.

Ready to tell on her. Lily has control of her emotions. However, at this moment. She is thinking. She wants to rip him apart.

All the evil. He has done and is still doing. However, she knows that it would be the end for Martha. She knows that he will make sure of that.

She has seen this throughout her investigations. Evil men will make sure the innocence of a child will pay. She knows that they need to die, but the law sanctions their behavior. Then they do it again. She thinks they should die.

Remembering the stories of the Gadianton Robbers. When she was a child. Hearing of the damage they caused as well. They ended, though.

No more to hurt for the little ones. She is thinking about all of this. She doesn't even see Sam's cousin. Not seeing the danger that lurked behind her.

He is so busy that he doesn't even notice her.

Lily takes a deep breath as she heads towards the file box. While she is heading there. She wonders what could be in there. Not knowing that it is a tell-all file in the box. At this time, Lily doesn't know this.

The file box took up one side of the room. Lily knows that this is so important. To the sex trafficking trade. As she looks at it, she knows that it could be a tell-all.

About each person they have sold and where they are. Each one tagged like you would an animal. It could even tell the name of the buyer. Knowing that she could see a few of the names.

Then noticing one name. He is the leader of the United States. Seeing that he is a big buyer. Sending them overseas.

Lily knows that she needs to get ahold of the undercover cop, but how? As she gets closer, she could also see.

There is a row of hooks for keys. She remembered. That each cage had a lock on the door. It clicked. These keys are for the locks on the cages.

Now Lily knows that this sex traffic ring needs to be shut down. The sooner, the better. And each one of these evil monsters. They need to be put away. Never to see daylight again.

With each step, she gets closer to the row of keys. She noticed numbers. Now she knows what they are for.

It hit Lily on the head. These little victims. Have no chance of getting away.

She just knows that there are parents out looking for their children. The pain of looking for a child. Not knowing where they are.

The closer she gets to the row of keys. Knowing that each number is a life. As she got there, she would stare at the keys.

Meanwhile, Sam's cousin is on the other side. Getting his poison ready to give to his victims.

Not knowing who could bring him down. Is standing steps away from him. To shake him down. Knowing her action could do this to him. Not knowing if it would work.

She gets ready to reach out. Just to get the keys quickly. With her heart beating so hard. She thought it would send her to her own gray world. As she reaches for the keys, a woman asks for her help. With a victim.

Lily knows at this moment that she needs to act. She just remembers that she has a cell phone. She could take pics. Of these keys and the names on the list. Also, pics of Sam's cousin. Being there and others. It needs to be quick. Just to make sure there is enough evidence. She takes the pictures secretly.

Grabs the keys with no one knowing what she just did. She couldn't get all.

Just one set of keys. Wishing that she could get all of them. Hoping that Martha is one of them.

She needs to come back to reality. Lily knows she needs to get out of there. She looks up and around. Lily notices Sam's cousin. Her heart is beating so hard. Lily knows that she needs to get herself under control. Her fear of him.

She wonders how she is going to get out of there. Without his seeing her.

Lily has the evidence to shut this sex trafficking down. If only she could get the undercover cop there. Not wanting any more victims.

Wondering if the police. Would get there in time. She must start thinking about getting out of there. Before she could get caught. How is she going to do that? Lily looks around.

Hoping that the tiny little camera. Could take good enough pictures. Knowing that she got caught. Everything is gone.

Seeing that Sam's cousin has his back towards her. The woman who needs her help. Also has her back towards her. Filling a case shot full of poison.

Ready to give it to a child so it could be ready for sale. As she slowly walks by, she takes pictures. She hears that there are three new girls who are ready to sell.

All they needed was a little poison to help. They need to do what the buyer wants.

Knowing that Martha could be one of those girls.

She needs to get to the door. Just a few more steps. She is hoping that she can get there in a few more steps.

Knowing they could stop her. They would check on her. Knowing they would have all the evidence.

She continues to pray as she gets to the door. Walks thru it. Knowing that she needs to find a hiding place.

She sees some wooden barrels with mental rings around them to hide behind.

Knowing the pictures she just took. Could blow this whole sex trafficking operation up. She knows that she needs to take a deep breath. Thank her Heavenly Father for watching over her. Catching her breath as she gets done thanking her heavenly father. She needs to move forward.

Knowing that she needs to keep going. Now, towards the cages.

Now she can take pictures of each child. Would she get to Martha before she gets the poison? Lily knows that if she gets it, she could be gone.

Either she could become addicted or die. Time is essential. She has a fear that she might lose this mission.

She knows that it can go badly for her. Knowing that her faith wavered.

She started quoting scriptures to herself. Knowing his promises are true. They are his covenant. Her strength restores.

Then Lily pushes forward. Knowing where she needs to go. Lily also thought that she needed to text the undercover cop. This would be the place. To text the picture, she took. Knowing that they would need it to get in.

Putting her little camera back in her pocket. While she remembers her piece. Just so she would be safe. She is hoping that no one saw her.

Leaving through the big white doors. Knowing for sure that if anyone saw her. It would be Sam's cousin. Knowing all would be lost

She heads toward the cages. Knowing that her heart would break. As she reaches the cages, she takes out her little camera. She takes pictures of the girls. Hoping that this would help the law. Knowing they could get away with all of it.

Lily would like the law to line them up and take their light out of their eyes. To have lives end. This evil deed is gone. Lily knows that her mind is doing its wandering again.

Her mind needs to be on its task. She knows that she needs to win this one for Martha and her. Then she can be done with this lifestyle.

She tries to continue, moving to each cage. Wondering if she ever would. Get to Martha.

Not knowing that, Martha. Is getting ready for her day view. With each cage Lily gets sicker. Knowing their lives will never be the same. Some will come out of this evil, and some never will.

Knowing that each child that she sees is a child of God. Heavenly Father's heart must be breaking. Lily knows that she has to stop thinking about this.

It's going to take control of her. The anger is filling her. Lily knows that she can't save everyone. While she is crying on the inside of herself.

Lily continues to go to every cage. Seeing each girl and boy poisoned. To have them not fight back. These children ranged from babies through twelve.

Suddenly there is a slamming of a door. Lily knows that this isn't good. She knows she needs to hide, but where?

Lily's heart skipped a beat knowing that. She has come too far to get caught.

She notices a truck parked over in the corner. It is kind of hard to see. As she got closer to it, she noticed that it was empty. It looks like an old beat-up army truck.

One that would carry soldiers. Lily would know this, because she rode in them several times.

Knowing that she could hide there. At least until the traffic is gone. She knows that she would be safer there. Then out in the open.

Knowing that these people are in white coats. Could know their own. She isn't one of them.

She wouldn't do this to innocent people. Lily wants to be one of the good guys. All of this evil is making her sick to her stomach.

As she gets to the truck, she puts her back. Towards the cab, looking around. Just to see what could be coming. Not knowing what could be around the corner.

Knowing that anyone that coming around the other side of the truck. Knowing this would be the end for her. She knows that being under the truck would be safer. She learns this in action before.

Under the truck, you could see everything going on. Lily knows that it isn't safe. She watches people walk by. Even the buyer. They are there to buy this little innocent profit.

How much could they bring in from their clients? Lily watches cautiously. Just to make sure she doesn't get caught.

She could hear. Some wrestling sounds behind her. Knowing that things could go badly fast. Her heart drops to her feet. Not knowing what could happen next.

She takes a deep breath. Knowing that it might help her. She looks around more intensely. Just to make sure that no one knows she is ready to be caught.

She is in a high state of investigation. Anyone there could stop here. She knows this.

This place is supposed to be vacant. Not a sex trafficking business. As she keeps looking, hoping that this will end soon. Trying to be aware of her surroundings.

Knowing that by watching. She can be ready for what comes along. As she kept thinking to herself, she could hear this growling noise.

She just keeps hearing it. She looks in the back. Just to see where it could have come from. Not knowing if it could be an animal. That could be ready to attack, for she is in his space.

CHAPTER 22

WILL FEAR TAKE OVER!

Meanwhile, Martha is trying her best not to give up. She knows that her options aren't good. Martha doesn't know what to do.

She remembers that her father taught her. How to pick locks. She knows that; she has a bobby pin in her pocket.

Martha knows that this is her chance to get out. However, she wants to save the little girl next to her. First, she knows that she needs to pick her lock first.

Would they come and get her first? Not knowing how evil works. They will make her do.

She knew that they gave this little girl poison. Martha reaches out to her, but nothing. She calls out to her, nothing.

Now Martha knows that she could be dead. For the past hour, she had seen girls come and go. They always came back. Like they are from a zombie movie. She doesn't want to be next.

She was becoming scared of what was coming. They will be here to get her soon.

As she put her hand in her pocket, she pulled two bobby pins out. Knowing that it took only one.

Knowing it could take a little more time. Then she is thinking it would be. Her heart is beating so hard. She could feel it. It is as if there is an earthquake in her body. Her hands shook so hard. She couldn't keep it in place. Just to unlatch the inside of the lock. Closing her eyes.

Seeing her mother telling her to pray for an opportunity. To try new things. When one thing doesn't work. Get on your knees. She could see her mother telling her this. Knowing that she needs to be calm. To unlock it.

She is an eleven-year-old who needs her father. She thinks about her father. Teaching her how to pick this lock. She can hear his voice. Cheering her on. Telling her she can do this. It is as if he is there. She knows that if he could be there. He would be there. However, he isn't here.

She knew that she needed to get out of there. She tries once more. The lock became free.

Now is her chance. She knows that people might be watching. Even thou she didn't see anyone. She slips the lock off and walks out of her cage. Not knowing they could see everything.

Looking and being on guard. Knowing that she needs to help this little eight-year-old girl out of her cage as well.

She needs to think about her father again to calm herself down. Knowing that she wants to save her. Martha didn't want her to die. Here in the last six hours, too much death.

Suddenly, she could hear voices. She knows that they are coming for her. As her heart beats to a drum, knowing that danger is coming for her.

She knows that it is time to go, but she wants to save this little girl first.

She is trying her best to unlock this stupid lock. Sticking the bobby pin. Moving it back and forth. As she frantically tries her best. Knowing that she could get caught. She takes a deep breath. Think for a moment. She needs to be calm herself, but how? The only person who could calm her down was her father.

She thinks about him. How could he wait for her to walk in the door? Then, her brother came into her memory. Her eyes filled with wetness. She knows that her brother is gone, and she could be next.

Martha looks at this little girl. Knowing that if she doesn't get out of there soon. She will die as well. Just like her brother. Martha calms herself down enough. To pick the lock the right way. Looking over her shoulder. Knowing they could be there at any time.

She wants to save this little girl. Even thou it will slow her down. Finally, the lock pops open. Throws it down, as of rebellion.

She walks over to the little girl. Tries to wake her. It is as though there were no life in her. Martha didn't know what to do.

She knows that she needs to get out of there. They should be there anytime. Her mind went back to a T.V. show. How a boy drug a person across the floor to get help.

Martha didn't know if this would work, but it is the only thing. She can think of at this moment. Grabbing this little girl by the trunk of her body, and pulled her out of the cage.

She stops to find a place to hide. As she looks around, she sees people in white coats heading her way. She could see them coming. Martha knows now that she needs to go.

She notices a dark closet. In the back part of the room. She grabs the little girl around the trunk and drags towards the closet. Now that they could find her easily.

Martha didn't know where else to go. They are coming towards her. She tries her best to shut the door quietly. While her heart thumps to the tune of dome. Martha hurries and places the little girl down. She sits down beside the little girl. Check to see if she is breathing. Her breath is very shallow. Watching the light under the door. Knowing they are out there.

Martha knows that she needs help. She knows that prayer works. She prays for the girl, and for herself, to get out safely.

Her father told her. That you are in trouble. Pray about it. This is what she is doing. She knows that they are in danger. Her father would always tell her he will always answer prayer.

Heavenly Father is here, and he knows what is happening. Martha bows her head as an innocent child would. Looking towards the heavens. With hands folded. Shaking in fear. Not knowing what is to come.

As she hugs the little girl, knowing that her Heavenly Father's got this. She knows that she could die at the hands of these people. Thinking that the little girl she is hugging could be dead. Knowing that, she continues hugging her and praying. Martha begs Heavenly Father for her and for their safety. While she is praying.

Shadows of feet, she could see. Under the doorway. She could also hear their voices. She knows they are looking for her.

As she holds her breath, the little girl finally takes a deep breath. They heard it. Martha prays that they move on. If only they hadn't heard it. This is their doom.

They know where she is. As they opened the door, they saw two girls. Martha knows that it is over. They would use her innocence and then sell her. Martha froze in fear. Looking at them. Hoping they would be easy on her.

One young lady. She recognized. This young lady is the one who brought her here. Then behind her is her father's cousin. Martha knows that it is over.

The young lady picks up the little girl and carries her back to the cage. Knowing that she needs to see a doctor.

As Martha looks at him in fear, he grabs her. By the arm. Grabbing and squeezing at the same time. The pain of his squeezing so tight. Traveled into the neck.

Martha had her eyes wet. As the wet droplets fall from her face, knowing that it is over. They won the battle. As, Sam's cousin reached the cage. He throws her in. Looks at her. "Tell her your next." "For the poison I have for you." "You will have a new owner soon," with an evil grin.

With a look of confession, not understanding what he means. He walks out of the cage.

A person in a white coat walks in. Martha looks at her in fear. The lady brings out a needle. Getting ready to poke Martha with it. Martha fought all the way. Kicking her feet and punching. Not wanting to get poked. Knowing what is going to happen.

Sam's cousin walks over and swings at her. She could feel a powerful connection. He hits her with such force. She hit the back of her head. On the bed frame. She falls into darkness.

Giving her his poison now would be a bad thing. Her being in the dark world would send her there for eternity. Never to come back. He doesn't want her gone. He knows he could get an acceptable price for her. Her beauty and her green eyes are priceless.

His cousin wants Sam to suffer like he is. He lost his little girl, so he should too. Not knowing where she is. Will haunt Sam more than anything else.

He ties her hands and feet to the bedpost. Knowing that now, she can't fight him. He will be able himself to give his poison to her.

There will be no way that she could stop him now. He knows that she might not be ready. To sell yet.

However, he knows that he needs to try.

The buyer wants to buy these young girls and boys. They are eager to pay top dollar.

Then he thinks. That this could be his daughter.

Knowing it isn't. Hating his cousin for having it all. He wants to get even with Sam for ruining his life. As he stays there, he keeps watching Martha.

Wondering if she is going to wake soon. He sits beside her, wondering if Sam has a clue. That he has her.

Martha woke with a moan.

Knowing that she is alive. Better than some girls. As he looks at her. He tells her, "Know you will be ready for sale."

As he leans over, Martha feels a poke. Sam's cousin gets up. Head towards the door of the cage. As he gets to the doorway, he leans over.

Tells the lady in a white coat. Get her ready for the buyer. We should get a good price for her. Martha knows her life isn't hers anymore.

No more dreams. She even wondered what it would be like to be dead.

Martha felt as if she were floating to another world. She feels as though she could be a fairy. Flying away from the cares of the world. Not having any clue. About what just happened to her. As one man comes in to pick her up.

Her head is hanging over his forearm. While her head bobs up and down.

He gets to a big room with a stage. Those six girls and two boys are sitting there. Martha has no clue why? She is Elven years old. Being sold as an animal.

Sam's cousin comes into the room. Tells the buyer that the bidding is starting.

Starting with a four-year-old. Not knowing that there is an undercover cop. In front row. Recording everything. Seeing this four-year-old. He becomes angry. Not showing it. Just to have this sex ring end in their town.

He recognizing Martha. Knowing that he needs to bid the highest for her.

CHAPTER 23

THEY ARE COMING!

As the uncover cop kept recording, the SWAT team was on the move.

While they move forward. Getting ready to end this evil. Making sure their guns are ready to free these innocent children. As they creep through the black tunnels under the car dealership. No one knows they are there.

In the darkness, they pressed forward. Knowing that there are lives that depend on them. Just to save them. Suddenly they come to some stairs.

As they climb them, being quiet. Taking them one by one. Knowing that they can be as a ghost. Going in and out of the wall. Knowing that they want to surprise their enemy.

As they get to the top, checking the doorway. One Swat member sees a guard.

Walking back and forth. The SWAT officer knows he is going to have to use force.

As the guard turns his back and walks down the hall. The SWAT member sprang into action. Knowing he needs to be a ghost. To surprise him.

Knowing that the light of his eyes could leave him. Still so willing to sacrifice his life.

As he springs into action. Knowing by the crack of his neck. He was gone. Leaving his body there and moved on.

The other followed him. Into an enormous room. The whole Swat team is in such shock. As they look, they can see rows of cages.

In these cages are children. They know that this is bad. They are to stop this from happening in their town.

As they kept looking, they could see babies.

Some of the SWAT team got sick. To see such evil. Now they could see why they were there.

Captain tells them, "Touch nothing." "We need to get these evil men." "We will need a few men here." "Then the rest with me." "The ones that are with me." "Let go now."

CHAPTER 24

GOT TO SAVE MARTHA!

Sam's cousin looks at him. With not seeing clearly. Sam could see clearly. For the first time, Sam realizes that his cousin has become evil. He has chosen his fate. Sam's heart is breaking because of his cousin's choices. That his cousin is making.

Sam's body let him know that he was done, for now.

His mind goes back to his daughter. He knows that Martha isn't safe.

Even thou his body doesn't want to work with him. He stumbles out the door. As quiet as he can, hoping not to draw attention to himself. His body wants to sleep. He thinks he needs to rest. Trying to find a place to hide. Trying his best to walk as if nothing was wrong.

Seeing people in white. Not knowing why? Wondering if these people could help him. Not wanting to talk to anyone because of the danger.

He just didn't want anyone to know that he is there. As he looks around for a place, he spots a hole that looks like a cave. Knowing that it could be a good place to hide.

He needs to get there first. He doesn't know whether he will make it. As his body is screaming at him, he walks fast as he can.

Knowing that, just a few more steps. He will be there. In a place to rest. He finally gets there. In the darkness. As he leans against the wall of rock. He thinks he will rest for a few moments. In the darkness.

Noticing that there isn't much room. Knowing he could see this big green truck. He recognizes it as one of the Army trucks. The color of khaki, an awful color. He rode in one a few times. When he was in Afghanistan, in the Army.

He needs to find a place to hide now.

Then it came into his brain. He could hide under the army truck. It would be hard for them to see him. He knows that the truck is tall enough for him to hide and be safe.

Knowing that he will be in danger. If he doesn't hide now. He knows that his body is going to give out. Then they will find him, so he crawls. Just to get under the truck. Hoping not to hit his head.

Knowing that it wouldn't be a good thing for them to find him lying there. Before he hides.

Knowing that in the Army. There were times you had to jump in. To save your brother in arms.

He would take a leap of faith. He knows that now is a good time to take the leap of faith. Before, they see him.

He knows that these are evil people. They wouldn't think twice. They would kill him first, then ask questions.

Martha is going to be on his mind. He needs to find her now. Blaming himself for the danger she is in. Hating himself for not pushing forward.

How his body does not agree with him. His body will not hold out. No more time. It is done. As he lay down in the dark, his eyes closed.

He heads toward the gray world. Fighting all the way. However, no more fight in him.

The gray world has won. It took over him. Not knowing when he will leave. Not being able to fight back. Sam does not know what is happening close to him.

Martha is trying to save a little girl. Within the closet. Not hearing her screams of pain meant there was no rescue. Which could be a few steps away. Sam isn't in this world now. Sam couldn't even save himself.

CHAPTER 25

QUESTIONING FAITH!

Meanwhile, Terry is standing by his truck. Praying to Heavenly Father. Stressed out, knowing that Sam is also in danger. Hoping that Lily finds him before his cousin does.

Knowing that Sam will do all he can to save his daughter. While Terry paces back and forth. Wearing out the dirt where he stands. Thinking to himself.

He knows that his faith is wavering. His faith has always been so strong. But now he is questioning his faith. Why would his heavenly Father do this to him?

Just to watch his friend go through this. What did Sam do to deserve this? Why is this happening to this family? Frist, his friend's wife has a stillborn baby. Then his son dies, then his friend's cousin takes his daughter.

What else is going to happen to this family?

As he keeps pacing, back and forth. *Wondering if his loved ones are safe. Not knowing whether they will make it.* He hangs his head downward. How his heart broke. The only thing he wants at this moment. *With his wife in his arms and his friend safe. Knowing that*

Martha needs to be safe as well. He keeps thinking that this whole thing is so bizarre.

As he gets ready to walk over to the Sheriff's car. He notices someone moving. In and out of the buildings. These people look as though they could be businesspeople. All of them wore business suits. All of them but one.

Also, noticing that there are some big white trucks, as if they are there to haul a large load. While he gets to the sheriff's car.

Terry let him know what he was seeing. Sheriff knows that Terry is worried about his friend and wife.

Even thou he knows that the professionals are in there. Still knowing that those large trucks are for large loads. They are going to move their victim. While he shakes his head. Once those trucks leave. They will be out of the country. His heart aches for them. Knowing that it all could go wrong.

While Terry prays under his breath. Knowing that just because he prays doesn't mean that it won't go bad. There are no guarantees in life.

He knows that you take it when you get it. He has to learn this through experience.

Terry has learned this from the death of his baby girl. He lost her. Now he could lose the other girl. In his life.

Terry knows that his Heavenly Father gave her to him. She is his queen. As he keeps trying to push, more positive to his brain.

Knowing that his faith is wavering. He is trying his best. Pleading to his Heavenly Father in his mind. *That his friend and wife are safe. Knowing that his Heavenly Father can be the only one that can do this.*

Terry's job at this moment is to keep the faith. A faith he has known since he was a teen. Suddenly, there is unconditional love. It hit him as if it were a mad truck.

Covering him from head to toe. It brought him to his knees. Knowing where it comes from.

He hears it in his mind and heart. That is his Heavenly Father. Is letting him know that he is in charge. That it is according to his plan, not Terry's.

How the Heavenly Father is unconditionally loving him by telling him. He loves his children, and this will pass. Telling him all of this. In his mind and heart.

Terry tried his best not to lose it. His face showed what he had just experienced. His face is glowing. He gets it. He humbly thanks his Heavenly Father.

Knowing that he is in a dark place. His faith is wavering. Deep down, he knows this. He had just had an experience of peace. Everything will be fine.

While the sheriff is talking to him. Terry did not even realize it. While he is in another world.

With a confirmation. That his wife will be good. He has known in the past, but he knows that Heavenly Father. He let his children know that he is there. Just like a father would. Now that he has peace.

He knows that he needs to find out what. Is going on. With the sheriff. As the sheriff continues to talk to the other police officer.

Pointing towards the buildings on the other side. Terry is wondering. Does he even know what is going on? As he tries to keep in the action, he can see movement.

Smaller people were being moved into the white, enormous truck. Wondering what is happening over there. Telling the undercover cop. About all the movement. Knowing that, Lily. Could be on one of those trucks easily.

What about Sam? What is going on with him?

With all the passing out he has done. Is he safe? As he sat back watching, all the action unfolded. Not being able to do a thing. He feels so helpless.

Terry is a man of action. He wants to step in and save them. This time he has to wait. He knows what those trucks are for, and he knows what must be done.

He knows that the undercover cops need to step in now before the truck leaves. Sam knows that if they get the chance, to pull out. Those children won't have a chance. It's all about Martha now. This will affect so many families.

Terry continues talking to the other cops. Wondering when they are going to do something besides talking to one another. Terry wants action now. As he thinks to himself, he wants them to go in now.

Before anyone gets killed. As he is standing there listening to their little chit-chat. How are they going to conquer?

This evil in their town. They are going to go to save the innocent. Terry knows that this will not be easy. This evil business of sex trafficking. Is a worldwide evil.

Terry knows these young people. Become as animals. It takes all their sense of decency out of them. It strips them from the inside out. Some may never come out of it. It takes years of help.

He knows these cops. Know what they are doing. He just wants it to be over. He wants Lily back in his arms, safe. His friend Sam was safe, talking to him. Martha was back talking to her friends. Everyone is safe and sound.

As if nothing had happened. If only he could go back in time. Everything would be good. It is what it is. A lot of heartbreak.

How could everything have gone so wrong? Terry knows that he needs to help, but how?

He talks to the cops. Asking what he can do to help. Not knowing how he could? Wondering if he should even offer. Not knowing there are undercover cops already in there. Ready for action. Just to end the evil in their town.

Sam had no clue. How to end the evil. He left the action to Lily. When they were in the army.

While he keeps waiting. Cops keep talking to each other. Trying to figure which way would be better to go in. Just to win the war. That will break out. Terry knows that the only way he could be part of the action is ... He needs to be in there as well.

He needs to get the cops to let him go in with them. Even thou he has never been in the middle of the action. Listening to the cops talking back and forth. He wonders if it would be best to just listen to them first and then ask.

Knowing that the officers could say no, he needs to be ready for that answer. Wondering if they would say no.

Would he listen to that, or do what he is thinking of, anyway? He knows that this is how Martha got into this. Terry, most of the time, listens to the cops.

But this time, lives are in danger. One of them is his wife. The other one is his friend and daughter. How could help them?

Terry knows combat is not for him. His is in electronics. He could work on any electronics and get them to work correctly.

As the cops keep talking, Terry is trying to keep up with the conversation. Asking them if he can join them. They look at him. With a look of surprise. Wondering why he would even want to go with them. Not quite understanding why he would.

Not quite know about his wife and friend. They know about Martha but not the other people. One cop looks at him and tells him. "We can't take you with us, but you can help us here." "By helping us to read this old map of the building." "These maps are from the late 1800. When mine was going on." "We know that in this area you could get to the mine." "We don't have anyone who knows how to read these old papers."

Terry knows how to read them. His grandfather showed him how to read old maps. He also did this in the army. Old maps are his specialty. This is the way he could help.

Terry wants to help terribly. Terry agrees to stay and help. He knows that he can help this way. As he leans over, the Office's car. He reads the map.

Seeing a hidden tunnel. Letting the officer know about it, by pointing it out to them. Taking his finger, and showed it to them. Also, seeing some secret chambers. Wondering if the offices could see them.

He points them out so they could. Letting the officer know that they could be closed off.

But they need to check them out. When they go in. As the officers get ready to go in, he hands them a few pictures. Terry looks at one officer.

Please look out for my wife. She is in there somewhere. Trying to save an eleven-year-old girl. From an evil fate. Please also save my friend. He went in there to save his daughter. I will stay here and do my best. In reading these old maps. There are some hidden rooms. I will keep you inform, as I keep looking and reading. I will tell you where to go.

There are some rooms on the ground floor. Under the car shop. Just to hide the children. No one would know they are there. As Terry kept pointing, the map gave up its secrets.

The leader of the SWAT team. Looks at Terry. Asking him to help them save the innocent. Telling the SWAT team to get ready. As the SWAT team gets ready to move in.

Knowing that they need to keep in communication with Terry. He will be the one who will bring them back. He will lead them through. All the hidden rooms. Could have danger. Some might not come back.

The SWAT team didn't want any surprises. For lives could be in danger. These men have families at home. Terry will be their guide. He is telling them where to start. Knowing that every hidden room could be danger.

They all know that they need to be successful. This is only one sex ring in their city. There are many in the world. This is the beginning. A fight for their children.

As the leader of the SWAT team looks at Terry, he touches him on the shoulder. Let Terry know that they are brothers. The leader looked at Terry again and said, "Military is family." "No brother is left behind." Terry looked back and said, "I got you."

The SWAT team heads out. Not quite knowing what they could see. Not even knowing where to start. They head out towards the other side of the building. Heading toward a tunnel of darkness underground. Only seeing through the night goggles. They had on to see by.

It is so dark that it had become scary. These evil people, knowing they needed to set traps, let them know they were coming. The SWAT team watched through their night goggles. Seeing a trip Lazer. Waiting for them. Not knowing what could be around the corner.

Some men on the SWAT team are a little jumpy. Not knowing what will happen from one moment to the next.

Knowing that a shootout could happen at any time. The good guy, with the bad. As they keep listening to Terry's voice, telling them where to go. They have become more conscious. With each step. Knowing that danger is around the corner. No one is around. It is so quiet. It is eerie.

They walk slowly around each corner. Wondering if someone would jump out and start shooting. Just to warn the others. They keep walking.

While they are alert of their surroundings. Not knowing that evil is happening above them. Evil doer who heart, have become lost in evil deeds.

They know that they need to be ready to go above ground. As the leader, took his hand. Shook it to go forward with caution. The SWAT team did not know. As the leader talks to Terry, wondering why nobody is around.

Terry let him know that they were getting ready to come to an enormous room.

To Terry, it looks about as big as a football field. What could be there? To Terry, he couldn't understand why they would need a big place like that. He lets the leader know about it. Told them to be careful. Going in there.

Not knowing what is going to happen. Hoping to catch these evil people. Off guard. Before they could succeed in their plans.

Not knowing where they are. Knowing that they will not find them soon.

Worrying about their leaving the city. Before they could put them away. Just at that moment. Terry tells them that there is an upper level.

However, they would have to go through the large room first. Which is about half a mile down. As they keep walking, with a little fear of the unknown. The leader lets them know to be prepared. What could come their way?

The leader knows that the team needs to keep going in the right direction. He knows that Terry told him to go straight. Hoping that the team follows him. So, many tunnels.

He is telling the team with his hands to follow him. They need to head in that direction. While he waved his hand forward.

A soldier shakes within himself. Knowing this could go bad for him. He is trying not to show it. Not knowing what could lie ahead for him. He knows that he needs to move forward. With his team. He will sacrifice his life for his brother. At nineteen, he will die for the innocent.

The team will go together. First, they need to keep going. They will have to go through the enormous room. Just to get to the other level.

Knowing that evil has to be up there on the upper level. Telling them to be careful. The evil ones won't let the innocent go without a fight. Evil doesn't care. Who is in the way? Even if they had to kill the innocent, or you.

Terry told them to look out for Sam. Look out for his cousin as well. Sam's cousin is dangerous. He works for them. He will kill anyone. even you. Be careful around him. He also told them to find his Lily. Terry's wife. She could help.

Terry reminded himself to keep praying. That they would be safe. Evil will not win. These evil monsters can't win this. If they do? They will take this innocent soul. To a place of destruction. Innocent children's souls in darkness. Never coming back the same.

Evil will lose this one. The monster should pay for this. Terry becoming angry. With these evil men. It shows in his talking to the SWAT team. As the SWAT team leader, tries to calm him down a tab.

By telling him, we will stop them. As they get closer to the enormous room, they can smell the stench of urine. Wondering where it is coming from. The closer they got, the more powerful it became.

As they try to cover their noses, it overpowers them. Their eyes become an over power by the burning. Wondering what happen. Why is the urine so powerful?

They get closer to the room. Darkness blanketed the room. The team couldn't see their hand even in front of them. Wondering if there is a light switch. The leader told them to stop in a whisper.

He goes forward on his own. Wondering if he would lose his light in his eyes. However, they need light, know to see the way. They need to know what that smell is coming from.

The leader wants to know if there could be a lifeless body. Finding its way to decay. He knows that it could be a big chance. He tries to prepare himself.

Hoping that his men get ready to look at horror in the face. Having thoughts going through his mind. Wondering where the light is. As he tries to navigate through the darkness.

With a small light. Running into thing, as he goes. Not knowing what it is. As he bumps into something, it makes a moaning sound. He thinks to himself. *Could this be an animal in a cage? Putting up his light, towards the sound he is hearing.* Noticing that it is a child. Didn't look any older than eight. His heart drops to a heartbreak. Soon after he saw this, devastation set in.

He has a son of this age. He doesn't understand how people can do this. How could they do an evil thing like this? He and his team are going to put a stop to this, even if they die for this cause.

He continues to look around with his light. As, the smell of urine became stronger than before. Seeing multiple cages. Each one having a different size of children. Some as young as two. He knows that he needs to get on his team.

They need to work together to end this to save these innocent children. He has to go back to get help from his brothers.

As he went back, he could hear a small child saying, please don't go. I want to see my mommy, please! Take me to my mommy. Don't let them hurt me anymore, as he grips the cage wire in fear.

He could see the small child's fear. In his eyes. Telling the child. I need to go get some help. I will be back. He knows that for his safety he needs to be with his team.

Knowing that he wants to save this child, he could put this entire case down the toilet. If he doesn't follow protocol. He wants these guys to pay for the damage they did. He gets ready to bend over to tell the child. "I will be back." "With more help, I will come back for you."

The child cries. "Please don't leave me." "They will hurt me again." "I want my mommy." "I am safe with my mommy."

He could see the fear in the child's eyes. He knows that this is real life for this child. Once again, he looks at the child in the eyes. While the child keeps trying to grab him. With the desperation for freedom.

Just to be safe. In his mommy's arms. Knowing that is hard for the child to understand. He looked at him again and tells him, "I will be back."

Just at that moment. When he tells the child that he needs to go. To get help.

As the leader talked to Terry. Terry could hear a child in the background. Telling Terry that they will need a lot more help.

The sheriff is standing beside Terry. He hears the whole thing. With the child in the background as well. Knowing they will need all the manpower they can get.

CHAPTER 26

HUMAN BEING SOLD AS ANIMAL!

Meanwhile, Sam's cousin is ready to work on the buyer. He wants to sell the merchandise fast. Before anyone will know. He knows that he has warren out his welcome in this city. His major goal is heartbreak. Sam will pay.

He needed to move to another city to sell his poison and get more sex slaves. After he sells Martha, he is gone.

To hide in the world of evil. The first thing that he needs to do is get these buyers to buy all the merchandise. Just to get it out of the city. Once they have been sold, as if they are cattle.

They go in trucks in disguise. Taken all over the world. He thinks that no one would ever know that it started here. The first merchandise will be his cousin-child. The buyer will bid the highest for her. She had a look that men would want.

Then out of sight, out of mind. Sam will lose another child. This made him feel as if he could be a god. Sam will pay. As he begins the bedding, he starts with a seven-year-old boy.

There is an undercover cop bedding him. Knowing that every word being said is being recorded. Hoping that all of this is good for the courts. In the undercover mind.

Hopes that he will fry himself. Hoping he will say his name. He keeps asking his name repeatedly. Sam's cousin becomes annoyed with him. It is as if the undercover cop is mocking him.

Undercover cop knows he needs to stop and be more discreet. As he looks at the little boy, he notices. That the other buyers are holding out a tad bit.

They are looking at the girls. The girls' ages range from four to sixteen. His stomach wants to bring up the food that just went down. Undercover cops know that these girls are for sex trafficking. The boys are for free labor or both.

That this whole thing is a sex trafficking ring. Ready to be busted. As he gets ready to turn around, not notice Sam's cousin behind him. Looking at him. asks him, "Who sent you?"

Undercover cop, sweating a little, as one of the three others spoke up. "He is with me." "We work together." A female undercover cop comes into the conversation. Very attractive to the eye. Sam's cousin try's doing a little flirting. With her. Not realizing who she is.

Knowing that he liked what he saw. He tries his best to find out more about her. She looks at him. With a look of disgust. Sam's cousin asks her why she does this.

She looked at him and said, "It is big business." "You take the innocent and teach them." "Now we get them to surrender and be the robots that are in them." "You train them to do what the client wants." "Then, if you can't, you drug them." "With no question." "The younger, the better."

Deep down, her heart is aching for these children. Knowing they might save these innocent children.

She turns around to ask him. How many do you have for sale? As Sam's cousin reaches over to her, he notices that she is caring. He looked down and said to her. "I see that you have a bulge."

As she looked at him, and said, "yes I am carrying." "Is that a problem?" "I have a lot of enemies."

As he continues to look at her, he understands why. She would carry. He is getting a message that she is just there to buy young girls, nothing else.

He looks at her to tell her. You are missing out on me. I am great. She looks at him with disgust. He gets the message. She is not into him. He knows that she is there just for business.

That money is more important to him than the girl. They are just a moneymaker.

Just maybe, she would make some kind of deal. With him. To him, this will be satisfying.

Just to have her in a place where she would be in his hands. He traps her. He will love that. Then they could make a deal that he wants.

He doesn't know that he is being recorded. The evidence is piling up against him. Just to prove that he knows what he is doing.

As he gets closer to her, her skin crawls. She thinks to herself. How he is a creep. No rational thinking with him.

How would she be attracted to that? A soul that has become a father lies. Not knowing that he once lived for truth. How a soul could fall from grace.

Sam's cousin knows that the bidding needs to start. The conquest of her will have to wait.

Knowing that she will be a prize to win. However, business must start. He walks over to the merchandise.

Just to start the bidding. Walking by each one. Showing them off. Touching their faces. Lifting their chins. Show everything as if it were an animal.

Getting them ready for a sale. Standing them up as best as he can. Each girl wasn't there, but is there, physically.

However, the girls did not know what is going on. He bid the highest bid just to make a profit.

He starts with the four-year-olds, for he knows that the youngest are worth more. Four-year-old cries out for her mother. Sam's cousin slapped her across the face. Then says, "You shut up." "You will not speak until you have permission to." "Your mother is gone." "You are to please your master." "That is the one that buys you."

As the little girl looks at him, with droplets coming down on her cheeks. With a handprint on the side of her cheek. She tells him that her mother would tell her to speak her mind. He gets ready to hit her again.

While one buyer steps in. She looks him in the eye. While she could see. He has no soul, for it was dark. "Tells him to back off." With her teeth showing, as if she is ready to tear him apart. Just if she is an animal on the prey.

The way it looks to him. She is protecting her young. He remembers how that was, for that moment. *His mind goes back to his daughter.* The look on his face shows it. *He remembered a ghost.*

He shakes his head. To put him back into reality. He needs to remember. That his daughter is dead. He needs to move on.

He looks at the little girl. Back off her. Looks back at the women.

Looks at the back room, and in his mind could see. His daughter stood at the back of the room. Knowing that she was dead. This freaked him out. Knowing that she would be upset with him. Hurting other children. His taking away the innocence of a child. People like him did this to his daughter. They gave her the poison. Took her ghost from her.

Now she is in Heaven. Never to come to him again. He knows that she wouldn't want him to do this. However, he has become an angry man. With the people who took her, he has become one of them.

In a way. He likes them. Ready to devour the innocent. Martha is one of those innocent souls. As he keeps thinking, he is reminded that he was a family man.

How could he do this to his cousin? He is feeling some remorse for the things he is doing. However, not enough to quit.

He was becoming scared. Knowing what will happen to him. He looks around to see. All the damage he has caused. He has to get out of there, and now.

He runs toward the door. Not knowing that the undercover cop will stop him. As he gets there, she steps in front of the door. He didn't knew that she was an undercover cop. He just liked her, but at this moment.

His guilt has him frozen. It is if he can't move at all. He knew the God he served. Has stopped him now. Just to remind him that there is hope. In, the Heavenly Father he once knew.

He knows that if he would change his mind. Just to do the opposite. He knows that he would be in danger.

His boss would help him meet his maker. He looks at the woman who is trying to stop him. He tells her that there is an emergency. That he needs to be there.

He knows that by leaving. He just put his life in another person's hands.

Then he remembers Martha. She trusted him. He needs to save her for redemption. Maybe he might be good enough again. To be saved as well.

Seeing his daughter's soul in the back of the room. It shocked him to the core. Not knowing that this morning. The heat from the memory of his daughter. Would melt his ice heart. However, he knows that in order to save himself. He has to do the right thing.

That would be to get ahold of the authorities. Just to let them know. Where the sex trafficking ring is. That it has come to their town. He knows that he would have to take responsibility for what he did.

Then take the consequences that go with it. First, he needs to get Martha out of there. Then, call the authorities. Knowing where to put her for safekeeping.

He has a hiding place. He would hide there at times. Knowing that he needs to save Martha this time. He thinks to himself how could I do this to her? "She trusted me.

I once did right by people. I know that I have harmed a lot of souls. How can Heavenly Father want me back? I have done so many stupid things. I have done the evilest thing, to innocent souls. How could I ever make up for that?

The only way he knows that is right is to wait for the authorities. But he needs to first go back in there and get Martha. He should be able to slip in and get her.

With no problem. The worker knew him as a hardnose. Even cold hearted.

With his daughter's spirit showing up in the back room. Showing her disappointment in him. Is too much for him.

Doing all of this to show Heavenly Father. How angry he is with him for taking her. Now he sees that his daughter shows disappointment in her father. He failed her. In so many ways.

How could he even ask Heavenly Father for help? He sees no hope in him. He is dark; there is no good in him. Knowing that while he was walking. He is thinking of all this stuff.

His wife gave up on him long ago. The only one he had left was his daughter.

Knowing he has to go back to that evil room, but first makes a call. Tells them there is an emergency. To come and be ready to protect themselves. That their lives will be in danger. For the evil deed of sex trafficking. Has come to their town.

There will be a lot of children in cages. They need to come and save them. He hangs up. Then head back to the room where the bidding was going on. Not knowing that two undercover cops. Had the other buyer handcuffed. Sitting on the chairs.

Sam's cousin walks in not knowing what had just happened. He walks through the door. He can see the buyers sitting down on the chairs. The same ones that were used for the buyers.

He became very confused. I didn't know what had just happened. As he comes in, heading for Martha. Being stopped by the undercover cop as she steps in front of Martha.

All he knows is that he left everything was good.

Now he knows that they wouldn't make it out without him. He knows a back way. Just to get in and out. Through the tunnel system.

Martha does not know what is going on. She has poison in her. She will do anything. After he hit her. She still had the marks on her face. Her thoughts are nonexistent.

At this moment, he was thinking to himself. *Having no clue. He looks at her. She reminded him of his daughter before she died. He watched the light leave her eyes. She was so poisoned.*

The question he asks himself? *Why would I work for them? All the damage he did. He looks at Martha again, knowing that her parents* want her home.

Just as he would want his daughter. Safe and sound. He looks at the undercover cop and asks her. "Do you want to know? The ins and outs of this business." "I will tell you." Knowing who she is. That he needs to save himself. The sound of redemption.

"If you make sure that these innocent children." "Get to their homes safely." "I will show you."

"Tell Sam that I am sorry for being so evil." "I know that I won't make to jail." "If I do, it won't be long." "I will be gone." "My boss will make sure of that."

"I know that I won't be at peace until I help you." "You know that I am a monster, but this monster is trying to make it right." "I don't know how to do that." "Knowing that I have done so much evil." "How do I make it better?" "I have become so angry." "The way my daughter died." "I want to get even." "I know that I am a dead man." "I need to make it right for these innocent souls." So many have had their eyes dim out." "I didn't do it, but was a part of it." "I just saw the ghost of my daughter." "It hit me like a mad truck." "She knows what I have done."

While the undercover cop. Looks at him. She tells him. "Since you are cooperating with us." "We can put in a good word for you."

Sam's cousin looked at her and said, "I didn't start out this way." "I used to be a missionary." "The one true God." "Now I am nothing!"

"I know what I have done wrong." Hanging down his head, telling her. "Can't take back all the damage." Looking towards her again. He reminds her that these are buyers. They will do anything to get their merchandise. Out of the country. We have a few buyers who are in Congress. We even have a few on the President's cabinet. You see, no one can stop it. This is in so many countries. He looks at her with a stern look.

"We need to get them out of here." "I know where to take them." He looks at her in the eye. "You need to follow me." "I have some hidden tunnels." "Under the floor." "It is soundproof." "They won't be able to hear them." "You will know where they are." "Yes, I will." "I will show you." Wanting to work with them, for now. Still at the back of his mind. Wondering if he could get away with what he had done.

"I go down there all the time." "When I don't want to do a certain thing." "I missed out on a lot more than damage." "I know somebody." "They are lifeless."

Undercover cop asks, "Do you know where?" Sam's cousin nodded his head no, "but I know this." "You get in their way." "They will take the light from your eyes." "Then throw you away as you are trash." I had nothing to do with the bodies. The ones that had their light come out of their eyes.

One buyer looks at Sam's cousin. Just to spit on him. Then, she called him a traitor. They will come and take the light out of your eyes. Your family will pay. He looks at them. Just to let them know. His family isn't on this earth.

Sam's cousin knows that he has to make a choice. Will he work with the officer or save his life? He knows what he saw. His daughter.

Did his daughter come to save him? She is dead and not with him anymore.

He knows that deep down it is his fault, of what he has done.

However, he has been blaming Sam all this year. While his thoughts are trying to take over his brain.

He knows that his decisions will determine his consequences. He knows that he needs to shake it all off. How does he do this?

He needs to decide now.

Knowing that he needs to lead them down into the darkness. He will decide then.

First, he needs to take the victims to the dark tunnels. Where people lost their souls. The more he thinks about it. His heart skips. To a tune of despair.

He gets up off a chair. Left his head knowing this could go wrong for him. Hoping to make his little girl proud of him.

He takes a deep breath. Walks toward the door. Knowing this could be it for him.

Making sure the victims are on their way. Leaving on the truck for travel across seas.

Bending over to talk to the buyer. Gives her a wink. Telling her that. Everything will be good. Handed her a knife to free herself.

Officers not knowing what had just been done. Thinking that it could be done and save these kids. However, they didn't know what was coming.

CHAPTER 27

DESPERATE TO SAVE A CHILD!

Meanwhile, Lily keeps trying to find Martha. Not knowing soon, she will be on her way to another country. She will leave in a truck. Then would fly across the sea.

Checking each lock, the keys went to. Hoping that she could get to Martha. Pray for each one as she passes each one.

She could see each child and his or her desperation. To go home. To be safe.

Not knowing if she could save Martha before damage happens. Praying as she is going. Praying for each cage she passes. Knowing that there is damage within them, and her heartbreaks.

Thinking to herself. With each cage. How could these people be so evil? With the innocent.

Suddenly. She could hear some noise.

She could be in danger. Hoping and praying not to be seen.

She ducks down more, as if she is crawling. Just like a baby would do. Hoping this could work. Just not to be noticed.

She raises her head. Just know what is going on. It was quiet, to quit.

It sounds as if they are moving their victims. Just to give them more of their poison.

She sees some people in white coats. They are coming her way.

Her heart thumps so hard. She could feel it beating to a tune. While her red sticky liquid pumps through her veins. Letting her know. She is alive for now.

Knowing that she needs to find cover now.

She knows that she needs to find a place. Just to hide herself, but where? They are coming.

All she could see were rows of cages.

Bending downward and walking at a fast pace. Trying to get around to the other side.

Knowing the safest place was in the Army truck. Knowing that she was safer there. How could she leave?

It is her job. To do her best to find Martha. Even if she sacrifices herself. However, she must save the innocent.

So many children. Where did they come from? She keeps thinking to herself? How did people become so evil?

Knowing that she needs to find a safe place for a while. Just until these people leave.

Sneaking downward, thinking that she should take pictures. Just in case the courts would need them. People need to pay for the damage they are causing.

Lily knows that she needs to continue. Taking pictures. Be quiet as a mouse. She has a fear of being caught.

Knowing that the officers could be here soon. Not knowing the Swat team. Is under her. Ready to shoot the bad guys. Ready to save the innocent. Just to get the evil out of their city.

Knowing that she still needs to push forward. Just so she doesn't get caught.

Where is she? Hoping to help her. Knowing this could go so wrong. Knowing that she needs to keep the faith. Not to let it waver.

Knowing that now is the time to move forward.

Making sure she continues to get the proof. Just to put them away. Ducking downward, she peeked around the cages. Just to make sure the picture came out well. Then, she took pictures of the children.

She did not think that was being watched on camera. While she is going in and out of camera view.

Lily didn't think that anyone could see her. She became a ghost in the past. Not being seen. Her enemies never knew who she was.

However, this time they know who she is — trouble. They know that they need to get ready for her. Before their secret is out. Taking the innocent for their gain. She could take it all away.

They had no clue what was about to come down.

They know exactly where Lily was. With an urgency. They will trap her. Then fill her full of the poison that takes over the innocent. Then throw her away as if she were trash. No one ever knew what had happened to her.

Lily knows that someone must be watching her. She is having a feeling. Knowing that when she had this feeling. It is a warning. Know to get ready for danger. This is a warning. Danger was being set in motion.

Wondering how it will happen. Knowing that she gets caught. She is as good died.

At that moment she lefts her head. She could see this black, shiny thing. Not seeing it clearly at first. Straining her eyes. Then she knows what it is. A camera. She knows now that she is in trouble. The first thing she needs to do is cover that camera, but with what?

Thinking that she needs to get out of view. Knowing that they know where she is. Wondering if it would have been better if she had stayed over where the enormous truck was. Knowing that she was safe there.

Knowing that she needs to get out of there now. They are coming. She can see them. They are going to find her. They know where she is.

While she is seeking downward around cages. Noticing a doorway. A way to get away. Knowing that she needs to get there before they get to her. Hoping that they can't see her. Knowing that she could be safe in there.

While she is trying to get away. She thinks about Martha. *Wondering where she could be. She needs to be safe. If she can just get to her. She knows who has her.*

While she continues to head for the door, fast. Thinking that she needs to look like the workers. Just to blend in. She could get away.

Lily wondered if Terry ever got ahold of the officer. They should have been there by now.

Not knowing what was under her. Is bringing a war of good or evil. People will sacrifice their lives. Just to save the innocent.

Lily doesn't know what is about to happen. Her mind is on trying to save Martha and her.

She finally gets to the door. Opens it. She sees a hallway. Where it led, she doesn't know. She walks cautiously.

Holding on to her gun. Being prepared to shoot if she had to. Know that this could happen.

She keeps walking. Knowing that she could take someone's life today. To have someone light to leave their eyes.

That isn't what Lily would like to do. She would rather save someone instead.

Knowing that this could happen. She keeps walking. Noticing that there are just medical beds and monitors. Telling herself how odd this is.

Seeing nothing like this before. What are they for? She asks herself.

Then she got her answer. She sees what they are for. She walks on it.

While she is walking with gun ready to shoot. She could hear voices.

Noticing that in a room with two beds. Two young girls. With three men. Wanting to get them ready for sale. Getting ready to sail for man's pleasure.

Lily knows that she needs to record them of what they are saying. She gets down. Then, crawls towards the door. Open it quietly. The men did not know what had just happened.

The men said evil things to condemn themselves. Being put down as evidence. To make them pay for taking the innocent away.

Lily is proud of herself. Hoping she can get away with this. Adding it to the proof that she already has.

Knowing that the courts would add this. It would put them away for a long time. They wouldn't be able to hurt anyone anymore.

Knowing how dangers' this is. Dodging around doorframes. Squatting downward to not to be seen. With her heart beating to a tune of doom. Knowing that she needs to find a way out of this. Before it was too. Needing to hide, but where?

Knowing that there are other rooms. Lily looks around. Just to make sure that no one has seen her. Hiding out and getting the evil one caught in her trap. Knowing that this isn't Afghanistan.

Knowing by the screams of the little girls. She knows what is happening. She knows what she needs to do, save them. The innocent are being damaged.

She knows what she needs to do. Knowing that she is the only one there.

Not knowing that under her. Is coming salvation for the innocent?

Knowing that she needs to sneak up on these two men. Just to catch them by surprise. Knowing this could be the only way to save the girls. Knowing that it could go wrong at any time.

If she is going to save them. She needs to move now. Her heart thumped with anticipation.

Her body slipped through the doorway. Making sure her gun is ready to take a life.

Taking a deep breath. Ready to save those girls. Ready to give her life to save the innocent.

While listening to the screams of the innocent.

Lily is ready to go forward. Trying to be quiet.

She knows that they are looking for her. If they find her. She wouldn't be able to save anyone.

She quietly moved towards the head of the bed. Noticing that their attention is on getting the girls ready. Not even noticing Lily in the room.

Finding out when two people in white coats come by. Just to get help to find Lily. Knowing that they need to find her now.

They take one of the bigger men. The stronger one. Thinking that she would never be around there. Not knowing Lily. Is hearing everything. Recording everything.

Leaving one smaller man there for the girls. Not thinking that it is that important. To leave men there. When there could be trouble running around. Not knowing for sure. They want to send the best that they have.

Lily knows that this is irrational. On their part. She knows this is going to be easy for her.

While they are in the doorway. One peek back in. Tells the man left behind. Give them poison. Then join us for the search. Not knowing their mistake.

They walk out the doorway. Down the hallway.

The man was standing around a small table. With needles and small glass bottles. Per pairing, the poison to put in them. Being careful not to put too much in the needles. Knowing they are smaller. Then, most of the girls and boys that come in.

While he is filling the needles. Lily prays. That she can do this before damage happens to them. Knowing without Heavenly Father's help. This will all go wrong. Knowing that he is making his move towards. The girls. Lily knows that it is time.

THE REALITY OF EVIL IS HERE!

Meanwhile, with Sam. Grayness is coming upon him. Safe, so he thought. Under the Army truck. He is trying to fight the gray world coming for him. His daughter needs him.

However, he knows that he is failing. This world is coming for him. Even thou he wants to fight it. It becomes too much for his body.

While he asks Heavenly Father before it comes for him. To cover him.

Not knowing. While he was out, to the gray world. The people in white coats. Are looking for Lily.

Not knowing what is taking place or whether he could be safe. However, he heard sounds around him. The grayness was reaching out for him. He faded into the gray.

While he is fading. People with white coats. They are searching for the intruder. Searching in every place. Looking in each cage. Knowing that she is somewhere.

Not seeing Sam. He is in a safe place. The hand of safety was covering him.

They're passing him, not seeing them. Where there is darkness. Knowing that where no one could hide. Searching anything that moved.

Going to the next room and doing the same.

While Sam is safe. He is missing all the action with his daughter.

His being in the gray world. Trying to get out. Forcing himself to get to reality.

He forces himself to wake up. Shakes his head. Pinches himself. Slaps himself. Anyway, that he could get out of this gray world.

Just to save his family. Now is the time. Since they passed by him.

Coming back to reality. Knowing that they have no clue. He is there.

Knowing he could be in danger. Which means Martha could be as well. Sam gets out of his hiding spot. Knowing that he is in the open. Now, anything can happen. His life could be in danger.

He thinks to himself. *He needs to find Martha.*

Then he looks around. He sees little children of his Heavenly Father. In cages. Just as if they are animals. Even animals live better than this.

He sees row after row of them.

Sam sees so much evil. He becomes sick. With anger.

He moves forward. Knowing what he needs. To just keep moving.

As he keeps walking, his heart is breaking for these children. With each cage. They became younger.

While he comes to one cage. He sees a little boy. He looks like he could be the same age as his son. His heart sank. Wondering if his Heavenly Father has a place for such evil.

He knows that this little boy needs to be saved. Knowing that his daughter is in danger as well. Just by looking at these little angels.

Suddenly. Sam hears a noise behind him. Not knowing what it could be. He turns around.

It is not what he wants. A person with a white coat on. Getting ready to take one child. Out of the cage.

Just noticing Sam. Getting ready to call on his radio.

Sam is trying to get his gun out. Knowing that this is it.

CHAPTER 29

THE END WILL COME FOR ONE!

eanwhile, Lily knows that if she is going to save these girls. She needs to act now.

Knowing that this evil man is filling these needles. To poison these beautiful girls. Just for their clients. It's easier for them to handle and control their clients. That is all they are. To these evil men.

Knowing that these two girls could die. In the hands of this stranger.

Knowing that the motherly instance is coming out. Just as if she were an animal. Ready to rip him apart. To protect her young.

While this evil man. His back is to Lily. She knows that this is the time. To sneak up behind him. Just to surprise him.

She knew that if she hit him in the head. With her gun. It would put him down. Into sleep world.

Knowing that she needs to get out of her hiding place. Sneaking around the bed, from where she had come. Knowing that he could overpower her. If he just would not know that she is coming.

Knowing that she just could not have the act of surprise. On her side. He would be down.

Trying not to make a sound. Trying her best to make sure that everyone. Is safe. She springs into action. Surprising him as he turns around. With the poison in the needles. Having the needle towards his abdomen.

Lily not knowing what is about to happen.

She kicks the tray. Hoping to kick the poison. Away from the girls. Knowing that the banging sound could draw attention. To where they are. Knowing that back up could be there in seconds.

Trying to be quick about it. She didn't notice. He is staggering. With his head towards his abdomen.

Not knowing why at first?

She sees the needles. All four of them. He got twice of amount of poison.

She knows that it would be a matter of time for the poison. Is pumping through his veins.

She needs to get the girls know and get out. Before backup comes.

Trying to remove the straps quickly. On their feet, calves and arms. An I.V in the top of their hand. Just to make it easier to give them the poison.

Lily knows that she needs to hurry. However, the more she hurries, too much she becomes agitated. Then she makes mistakes.

While the evil man falls down. Knowing that he is having his life leave his eyes. He gives out a plead to help. Knowing that there is no hope for him. He lets her know how to remove the straps. With his last breath.

Lily realized she could not take her eyes off him. She knows that it is done.

Finally, the last strap is off. Now is the time to get out of there. Making sure her gun is in her gun holster. Just in case she needs it. Then, out of the area. They went.

First, Lily needs to make sure the coast is clear.

Not noticing that the girls aren't walking, they are crawling. Not very good at that either.

She knows that this isn't good. If they are going to get out of there. They need to be good enough to walk, maybe run.

Lily prays softly to herself. Knowing the reality of the danger. Has just intensified. Reminding her of what she has done for her country.

However, this is one for her friends.

Knowing that she needs to get her head back into reality.

While she is listening to the radio. In the background.

She has just realized. They are looking for her. Knowing that her life is in danger. More than the girls. They are their profit.

Knowing that they could come down there anytime. Just to find them.

Lily knows what would happen to the girls. She has to save them and get them to a safe place.

She gets to the doorway knowing she could hear voices. Knowing they are coming.

With her heart pumping her red sticky liquid. Beating a tune of fear. She moves forward with the girl. Who are around the ages of six or seven?

Having both hands full. One with her gun ready to take a life to save the innocent. Having the other hand full of the innocence of a child. Leading to safety.

Knowing that any wrong was on her part. It would be over for them. Praying under her breath, for them to be hidden from the enemy. While they move forward. Trying to do it quietly.

Walking with caution. Looking in every room down the hall.

Just to check, for more innocent children. Waiting to be rescued. Not knowing if she could. To save them as well.

Checking each room. When she goes by. Just those evil men couldn't stop her.

Knowing that she is getting closer to the end of the hall. She becomes aware. She will be in the open of danger.

Lily turns around, trying to make sure the girls are behind her.

Knowing that she is going to find a place that would be safe for them. There is still too much poison in them. Still not walking well. They are not in the real world yet.

She notices they are getting better, but not there yet. Just to make sure they are safe. She needs to hide them. Then, she will need to move forward.

While she is not forgetting Martha. Her mission is to save her.

Knowing that the hallway is going to end. She needs a plan. What is she going to do? While she keeps thinking to herself.

She knows that first thing. Hide these girls. Then, she needs to find Martha.

She knows that she needs to keep pushing forward. Her faith is wavering. Just as If, she is on the water of the ocean. Lily needs to find her faith. She wonders if she is losing it. She is wondering all of this while she keeps looking.

These girls are her responsibility.

Lily doesn't know if the law is there. Will they help her? Not knowing if she would come out alive. She is going to do her best to save them.

Thinking that she is the only one there. Realizing that she is in a deep sex traffic ring. People don't make it out.

She keeps walking. Looking while she goes. She sees a room with a large closet. With a place to hide.

Her heart beats to the tune of doom. Knowing this, was the only place she could find. Praying under her breath, for safety for them. Until she gets back.

Lily gathers the girls. Walks through the doorway. Towards the large closet.

Opens it up and finds the dead body of a child. Screaming while looking, noticing. He is a young boy. The same age as Steven. Being sick of what she is seeing.

The way the body is damaged. She knows what has happened to him. Someone has used him in their sickness.

Know that the same thing could happen to the girl. Knowing that the girls need a safe place.

Lily grabs the girl's hands. Walking away from the body. Knowing who killed this little angel. Will be back to get the body.

She has to keep going.

Grabbing the girl's hands. Just to walk out the door. Trying to find another place of safety.

Knowing that this could happen to them.

This made Lily angry. How could someone do this to a child?

This means war now to her.

She thinks to herself. *Put these kids in a safe place. Then, get rid of the evil men. That are damaging the innocent.*

Thinking that she had a phone. For a moment she forgot she had a phone.

Wondering if she had a signal. Just to call her husband to see if she could get some help. Just to bring these evil men down.

Then she heard something. It is voices. Trying to hide by the doorway of the room they are in. Making sure the girls are quiet. Just so they don't give away their spots. Knowing that they are vulnerable. To the evil, man's abuse. Maybe even death.

It is time for Lily to use her training. To take lives.

She didn't like this part of her job.

Putting the girls in the closet. Just so they wouldn't see the carnage. She will have to do. Not knowing what she might find in the hall.

Waiting for the right moment. To come out. With the mark of damage.

Her aim has to be good enough to put her enemy down

CHAPTER 30

KNOW THEM BY THEIR ACTIONS!

Meanwhile, Sam's cousin. Is leading an undercover officer down through a tunnel. Knowing that he is leading them. To get caught by evil men.

To put them with the fishes. Just so no one would know his evil plan. At this moment, he is deciding.

He knows that his daughter. Wouldn't be happy. With what he is about to do. However, he also knows. If he does the right thing. They would take the light out of his eyes. He would join his daughter.

As he keeps walking down the tunnel, he hopes. Asking Heavenly Father for help. He knows that he has done wrong. Wanting to make it right. Just not knowing how.

Knowing soon he needs to decide. The tunnel is ending. At the end of the tunnel. Is an enormous room with more innocent children.

It would be a perfect place for him to decide.

He turns toward Martha. While he looked at Martha. He could see the poison. Wear off. Her eyes are becoming clear.

She knows who he is. She knows what he is. Her father has been right all along. She looks through him, as if all she sees is nothing, and that scares her.

Still feeling as if she got run over by a truck. She sees a lot more clearly. Knowing that she is among children younger than her. *Thinking to herself. She needs to get out of there.*

The more she looks around. She understands. While she continues to think to herself.

Knowing that she was to be sold. Just moments ago. Knowing that something has stopped the sale, but what?

While she keeps thinking to herself.

She noticed Sam's cousin.

Her mind became clear. It was fuzzy before, but now it is back.

She does not know what is about to happen.

She looks down into the abyss. Knowing that her life and all the victims. Are at the mercy of their owners.

As she looks downward, she notices. A little girl. Coming out of her poison.

While she keeps looking at her. Knowing that she couldn't be any older than four.

She does not understand why she is there.

Martha looks up towards the sky. Her father's cousin.

Knowing in her heart. She could feel a chill from him. Knowing that she needs to get away from him. He won't let her go. She knows. He would hurt her if he could.

Thinking to herself. *Just at the moment of despair. She remembers. What Lily told her. When she was sitting at the funeral place. As they sat on the chair talking, waiting for her father.*

Lily told her to always remember this, to pray about it. Heavenly Father always listens to his children. He will always give a way out.

She knows that she needs a way out now. She just wants to go home.

While she prays, to herself. Not having the faith yet. Being only eleven. Not understanding yet...

Looking around as she keeps praying to herself.

Knowing that she could lose her freedom, as a child. All she could feel. His doom will each step she took. Her faith as a child that once had. Is losing it.

She could see herself alone.

Thinking about her father and mother.

She lost her brother. Thinking that this is her fault. Just maybe this is her punishment. Maybe her life. Could end as well.

Knowing the tunnel. Is ending soon. Martha knows her life could end at any time.

Her heart beats to the tune of danger; everything spins. Just as if she is on a merry-go -round. Round repeatedly. Never to get off.

Knowing that she needs to sit down. Just to take a breath into her lungs. While she stops for a moment. One of the undercover officers. Stops to ask her. Are you okay?

While she is rubbing her shoulder.

Knowing Martha, she must be terrified. She is a child.

Sam's cousin is trying to look as if he is trying to help. However, deep down he isn't. He is trying to find a way out. Just to save his own neck.

He is trying to go behind the group. Hoping that no one will notice. Him gone. Until he is safe.

Not knowing that one of the undercover officers stays farther back from the group. Just for this reason. They couldn't trust him.

After the undercover officer. Saw him give the buyer a knife. Just to save themselves. They knew that he would do whatever it took to save himself.

While Sam's cousin try's sneaking backward. Not wanting to be noticed. He backs up onto one of the undercover officers.

The officer pushes forward. Making sure he moves forward. Knowing what he is about to do.

As she moves him forward, she hears something behind her. Knowing that the girls are ahead of her.

This is a warning. They need to hide- and NOW!

They must save these innocent children. If they are to lose them. They will be lost. Just as if they were yesterday's trash.

While she keeps thinking to herself. She knows that; she needs to move these girls now.

While she tries doing hand signals. Trying to get their attention.

Just to help get to safety. Not knowing what could come to them.

Knowing that their lives could be in danger.

As one officer looks, she notices. That some girls are doing well. Then a few aren't.

They will have to find a place for the innocent girls. That can't move forward. Until they do.

Leaving an officer with them. Just to protect and sure they are safe.

They know who is best one is to do that. An officer who works with children.

Both of the officer's look. To the third officer. They both know who is to do that.

As the third officer looks at them, he nods his head. He tells them to go.

While they try to find a place to hide with the victims.

They know the time. Isn't on their side. They continue to look.

He finds a room, but it is locked. Knowing that he has to break the glass to unlock the door.

Opening the door. Just to see where and how they would hide. Seeing a table in the corner. A small closet is in the corner. On the other side of the room.

Knowing that this could work for them.

Sending the other two offices. Moving forward with the other children.

He will protect these innocent victims. He will die for them.

Knowing that he has to move, the children know. Before danger comes.

Moving them one by one. Now that time is very important. Each one isn't able to walk. He picks them up one by one. Sit them down in the corner. By the closet. It is out of view of the door.

They would be safe there. Bending down forward. Let them know that they are going to be okay.

The more he looks at the victims. His heart tries not to break. Some victims are so young. Only three or four years old.

Knowing that he needs to watch out. For the evil men.

He would wait for them. Watching at the door for them. Being an expert marksman. In shooting his mark.

Leaning up against the door frame. Waiting for the enemy to come through.

Knowing that his 3-57, Magnum Revolvers.

He has only six rounds. He knows that isn't much.

They will come soon for the innocent. They will want their profit.

Meanwhile, the other victim. Are walking down the dark tunnel.

Making sure they walk in single file. One officer in front and one in back.

Just to make sure they are safe. Just in case. Knowing they had to keep going.

They can hear a voice. Not knowing where. The tunnel is carrying the sound.

They keep going. Trying not to breathe loudly. Knowing that their sound could carry and let the enemy know. They are there.

They reach the end of the tunnel. The victims became a statue in fear. Getting them to calm down is work. The office knows that this is devastating. To these victims.

However, they need to calm them down to move them to safety.

Knowing that the tunnel is ending, they need to find shelter. Before they go into battle.

Both of the officers look around. Noticing that Sam's cousin isn't around. Knowing that he snuck out of there.

Hoping that back up could catch him.

Knowing that they are to text their leader. They need to text them anyway. Just so they could have their back. To come and help. Not knowing what is about to happen.

Knowing that a SWAT team has been called.

While they are texting. One officer. Could see one man pointing a gun. At another man. He is just standing there. With his hands up, as if he is reaching for something.

One officer sprang into action. She just knows. In order to save his life. She must stop the man with the gun.

Knowing that at any moment. He could turn around and kill her. With just one shot.

Trying her best to be as quiet as a church mouse. To stop him before he could stop her. Quickly moving up from behind. Making sure she is in position. To drop him. If she has to.

Telling him to drop his gun, or she will shoot him.

Sam knows that she saved him. He is so thankful to her. She came at the right time. Knowing that it could have. Went the wrong way.

He goes toward the officer. She looks at him. Tells to stop. She drew her gun on him.

Sam stopped and understood why. He knows the drill. He takes his gun. Lays it down on the floor. Knowing that he is at the mercy of the officer.

Sam has one mission. To save his daughter. However, he needs to do more. So many victims. Children like his own.

The other officer had the innocent victims. Making sure they stay where they are.

Not knowing that Martha just recognized. Her Father. Sam weeps. He knows that his daughter is alive and well, for now.

They run to each other. Just to embrace each other. Knowing that they are alive.

Everyone needs to work together to get out alive. Not knowing what might happen next. Knowing that their live are in danger.

Not knowing they are being watched. They know where they are. War will come to them.

Sam spoke to the undercover officer. Trying to find a way out with the victims.

Making sure the perimeter is clear. Knowing that there has to be a way to get ahold of the outside.

Undercover officer has a radio. She is talking to someone on the other side.

Sam recognizes the voice. *It sounds as if it could be Terry. But no, Sam thinks to himself. This couldn't be.*

Then he thinks a little more. Then he remembers. Terry did this in the army. He would read maps. Then, guide the troop through the maze. Just to make sure of the troop. Could live another day.

Then Sam got an idea. If this is Terry. Then he needs to let him know that him and Martha are okay.

They did a perimeter where they are. It is all clear.

Describing the area. Rows and rows of cages. With innocent victims. Not seeing any camas, so they thought. That they can see.

Sam continues to tell him what it looks like. How there is three ways to get in. This large room. Which is so huge.

Letting him know. The SWAT team needs to get there soon. All these victims need to be rescued. So many victims.

Where will all the help come from? All victims are going to need help.

Sam continues to talk to Terry. Just to find out there is a SWAT team coming in.

Not knowing that the evil men could hear everything being said. They are coming to take their property back.

CHAPTER 31

COMING TO SAVE!

eanwhile, the SWAT team could hear everything happening. As they keep going. They come to three tunnels. Not knowing which one to take.

The captain divides them into three groups. Each one has a leader. That has been in battle before.

Each group takes a different tunnel. Knowing that now, silence is a way of living. In this moment, each officer's life is on the line. Knowing that they can lose it.

Knowing their hand signals. Are very important. Any sound could give them away. Making sure they have their earpieces. In their ear. Phones in silence.

Making sure of their night goggles. Could see everything. Any adult could be their target.

They trudge through the tunnels. Trying not to draw attention to themselves.

Knowing that the victims are at the end of the tunnel.

Terry kept in touch with them. Reading the map to them. Let them know how far they need to go. In code. Each song meant something.

Knowing that his wife is in danger. Hoping she is safe.

Praying to himself as he reads the map.

While he read to them. He could see that one tunnel had an exit door. Not big. But big enough to get out. With no one knowing. An escape hatch.

Let them know that they need to send some officers. Over there to watch the door. Just to catch whoever comes out.

Knowing evil men. Will try to flee. Just to not pay for their evil behavior. Terry knows that he / she / they might do this. *They will run.*

Knowing that he could see white trucks as well. Wondering if that could be where the exit is. To him, it seems like it is. Looking at the map. Studding it. Knowing that this could be the spot. Where they came and went.

Then, seeing a mark on the map. Knowing the sign. Showing a rap. While Terry continues thinking. Knowing this is how. They are moving the victims? With no witnesses. Moving them all over the world. Martha could have been one of them.

Knowing that the captain needs to know. As he shared what he was seeing, he could hear someone on the radio. Asking how far they have to go.

Terry asked with a code song. Knowing someone could be listening. On the line. Hoping to direct the officers. To where they could fight for the victims.

As he was trying to lead them, the officers could smell the stench of ammonia.

Terry knows they are there. Letting them know they are close. To keep their eyes open. The enemy of evil. Is at hand.

Terry knows that he needs to move on. To the next group of officers. He knows they will have to be back up.

He knows that all three tunnels lead to the enormous room. Right where the victims are.

He needs to lead them there.

Still wondering if his wife is alive. Knowing that she could have killed. He knows that she has dogged death before.

Then this feeling comes over him: she is alive.

Terry knows what this feeling is. It is the Holy Ghost. Letting him know. Now he knows that she is alive. Time to get back to the task.

Back at the looking map. Noticing another room under the ground. Just under the rap. Two more tunnels. Just be able to escape. Terry is finding more tunnels. More than officers. This isn't good. Calling over the captain. Just to come over to look at the map. Terry points out the multiple tunnels.

The captain knows that this is a war zone now. They need help. The National Guard. Time to call the governor. To call them in. Captain looks at Terry, just to tell him. This isn't over. This just became a war.

Terry knows. That it is time to call. His brothers in Christ. To gather in prayer. He knows in the scriptures, Matthew 8:20. When two or three are gathered in my name, I am in the midst of them.

Time to call all the churches in this town. Just to pray and fast, for this evil to end.

Terry never knew that evil had been here before. He had never heard of sex trafficking before. Never thought that it could be this close to home. He has known that it has been in other places. In other enormous cities, but not small towns.

He picks up the phone and calls. The leader of his church. Just to tell him what is happening. Terry asks him to get ahold of as many people as he can. They need a prayer group; you know. He tells him what is happening in their small community. Terry let them know.

They need help. They want to get the innocent out. Letting him know of the evil in their town. Telling him they need a miracle. Pray and fast for the safety of the children, as he tells him. Also, for the men and women who put their lives on the line. Just so our children can be safe. We need this miracle NOW!

While Terry is getting off the phone. The captain is on the phone. Calling the Governor. Just to bring in the National Guard. War will break out. In their town.

Captain tried his best. To just get the Governor to listen. About the danger. In their town. Evil is there. They need to cut it off. From their state.

Governor is shock. Just to hear of the evil. In his state. However, he couldn't send any help. The National Guard is on assignment. overseas. They wouldn't be back for another month.

The captain knows he is on his own. He knows they are going to have to make a plan. This sex trafficking ring. Needs to be stopped at all costs. Too much damage.

He looks at Terry. Just to tell him. We need a plan. "Are there any tunnels that are blocked?" And which one can we use to our advantage?

Terry knows that some might block. Some tunnels are big enough to drive trucks through. He would have to study it more.

Then Captain asks Terry, "Which tunnels could we blow up?" "Blow all of them but one." "Knowing that we could bring victims out of that tunnel,"

While Terry looks at him. An idea came to him. Looking back at the captain. "Why don't we keep two open?" "Then we could wait for the evil to come out." "Bring them into the open."

Captain knew every man. Will need to be on the job. Their job. Will be to protect this town. From evil doer.

Captain knows now that he needs to be with his brethren. He needs to go into the den of evil.

Just as he gets ready. He cocks his gun. Just getting it ready. Knows that he could take a life. He will have nightmares from doing this. He knows that this is what he does. To keep the street safe.

Just as he looks at the map one more time. Before he would go help his breath.

Just as he gets ready to head out. Detective Binder shows up.

Knowing that Binder had been an undercover detective for thirty years. Twenty has been involved in sex trafficking rings. He broke up sex rings overseas. Know that he has retired.

He heard it on the police scanner. The heartbreak that is happening in this small town. All the innocent victims. Knowing that he has to do something. He knows how to help.

As he walks closer to Captain, just to let him know. That he can help. He has done this before. Knowing what to do.

Telling him they need to be caught. While looking at the map.

While he looks at Terry. Let him know that he is going in as well. He looks for an earpiece. Cocks a heavy- barreled AR-15. A marksman's rifle. He knows these men will shoot to kill. They will take the victims with them.

Detective Binder continues to talk to Terry. Look at the map one last time. His finger points to the area he is going.

Down in a tunnel. Where no one thought of going. He looks at Terry and tells him. "This is where the leaders are. He points to a large place on the map."

"Send back up." "Then the SWAT team will need to be a backup as well." "Send half of them my way." "Then the other half." "To the victim.

Looking at the cops. "Letting them know that there will be some deaths."

Looking back at the captain. "Letting him know that he needs to stay." "Telling him that the men trust him." "Letting him know that they would follow him." "To the end of the world." "I will need you to guide them through."

"Our goal is to stop them from selling the victims." "They will send them across the world."

While Detective Binder looks at all the cops. Around him. Knowing that they need to go with him.

While Terry continues to look at the map. He sees a mark. Not knowing what it could be. Detective Binder was called and went over to look.

He knows what it is. He puts his head down. Terry could tell this isn't good. Detective Binder knows what this mark means. He lifts his head. With a crack in his voice.

People don't know this. In, sex trafficking rings, this is a place. Where they get dumped. When they are dead. Just as if they are trash.

He looks at Terry and tells him. I know where I need to go.

Making sure that he has a bulletproof vest on. Earpiece in his ear and another gun. Knowing that he needs his three fifty-seven Magnum with him.

War is going to break. Some will never come back from this. This is the part that would break his heart.

He looks at the map again. Knowing that this could be his last time. Remembering each detail. Making sure he remembers. Where he needs to be.

As Detective Binder turns around. Knowing that these men. Brave men. Might not come back. To their families. Knowing that he is going to take these officers. Into danger.

He looks at each one. Knowing that each one has a family.

While he could feel the thump of every beat of his heart. Carrying a tune, as it went. They are going to fight this evil battle. Knowing that they might not come back. They need to go NOW. First, he wants to let them know that there might be security cameras.

To be on the lookout for them. Also, be on the lookout for the Sawt Team. Hoping that the evil men don't know about them. Just to surprise. Knowing that once they are in. They are in danger.

Binder looks back at Terry and tells him, lead us through, please. I trust you. Then gather all the officers. Then head toward the north side of the building.

CHAPTER 32

DEATH IS COMING FOR THEM!

eanwhile, Lily is trying her best to keep the girls quiet. Knowing through the camera what she saw. In the room they were in. They know she is there. Knowing that they will be looking for her. They are in danger. Lily knows this, but the girls are too young to understand. She needs to get them out of the closet and find another place. Closer to where she needs to be. Knowing this could risk it all.

With every second. Her heart is telling her. The risk she is taking.

She knows that she needs to leave them there in the closet. However, she needs to keep going, but her body says no. She has to push herself forward.

Knowing whether she could keep walking down the hall. She might find a safer place to move them to.

She knows that she needs to head back to the large room. There is a place to hide and get help.

Her body is shaking with fear. Knowing that she might save no one. Her heart keeps in tune with her fear. It is playing its own song. She tries not to show it to the girls. She has taken out of the closet. Hoping to find another hiding place.

However, reality is coming to take its victims. Lily continues to save. Anyone who will need to be safe.

Her faith wavers. She asks her Heavenly Father for help. She knows that she can't do it by herself. Wondering if there is any help for her and the girls.

As she keeps looking around corners. Just to see if anyone is there. Just to do harm. To her and the girls. Checking each room, she passes them by. Not knowing whether she would shoot. Then give herself away.

Step by step. Quietly knowing and hoping this ends soon. She knows the risk.

Not feeling as if she would be alive from one moment to the next. Knowing what she needs. To keep them from being seen.

Not knowing that her life is in danger from a friend.

Lily knows as she comes up to a room that she saw earlier. This is the one. It has a large closet. She could hide the girls in there. They would be safe. Then she could move forward.

Getting to the room. Going through the door. Looking around the corner. Just to make sure that no one is there. Having the girls stay behind her. While she looks.

See that it is clear. She knows that this is the time to put them in the closet. Looking at them. "You are not to say anything." "No one is to know that you are here." 'If you do this.' You will be safe.

Lily moves them toward. The floor of the closet. Sits them down. Gives them two bottles of water. She carried with her. Knowing that they would need it.

Lily keeps hoping that they will be out of reality. Knowing that they are ready to see a dream for a while. Knowing their little hearts. I can't take much more heartbreak.

Leaning over, just to say a brief prayer for them. Then, they shut the doors. Knowing that their Heavenly Father will watch over them. Knowing that she needs to leave them.

Walking with each step. Knowing there is lurking. Around the corner. Getting to the doorway. Looking out to look for danger. Her heart is beating so hard she can hear its own tune.

Knowing that she needs to get out of there. She thinks about Martha. Wondering whether she is safe. With mind wandering, she knows she needs to get back to reality. Has she been sold? Knowing she could even. She could be on her way to another country.

Not knowing that she is safe with her father.

As she runs towards the hallway, she wonders. Is she ever going to see her family again? While she keeps moving.

She thinks. How could she see her leader? Her mentor. Come out of nowhere. The man who trained her in the Army. No, this can't be true. He wouldn't be here. Why would he be here? Then the figure of the man came forward.

Her heart becomes frightened. She knows who he is. She has an unpleasant look. On her face. She doesn't know now why he is there. However, she is going to find out.

As he moves towards her. Lily's heart pounds through her chest. It is at this moment she understands. Why he there? By the way, he carried his body. He is part of this evil. She knows now. She is a goner. With no place to go.

He comes after her. Not knowing the two girls. In the room she had just come out of. Lily will give herself up for them. Just to keep them safe.

Not quite understanding. Why would he do this? He has girls of his own.

He comes closer to her. Asking her why she is here. Inching closer to her.

Lily's heart is letting her know that her vein could burst. At any moment. Her fear is of reaching the top. Knowing that she could lose her life. Knowing he could be the one who takes it.

Praying to Heavenly Father, she said to herself. Knowing that he takes the light from her eyes. It is up to her Heavenly Father. Not knowing what could happen.

Knowing she has no place for her to flee. She put her faith in him so many times. She is here because he had saved her.

Lily trusted him with her life so many times. This is how he is going to take it.

She looks at him with a stern look. With her heart in sorrow. Just where she stands.

He has his hand. On his gun. Pointing toward the head. Lily takes a few steps towards him. With its red sticky liquid to remind her. What is to come?

She asking him. "How can you do this." "What would your girls say to their father?" "Why have you become so evil." "I trust you with my life." "If you can kill me." "Then there is no hope in this life."

Knowing that he could shoot her at any time. She keeps pushing him. Just like she has always done. Hope he would decide soon. Time is precious. Lives are at stake here.

With Lily being a redhead. Sometimes she didn't know when to keep her mouth shut.

Knowing this time. She could lose her life. She knows that his anger would get the best of him eventually. Knowing this, it could be to her advantage.

She thinks to herself. *Praying to herself, she is leading them away from the girl. Knowing that they are just a step away from them. Lily keeps thinking that if she could keep.*

She could get them out of the area. With her heart beating to a tune of doom. She could feel it as it filled her veins. She knows what is about to happen.

Knowing that she will become part of the trash soon. She will try to save these girls. She continues praying to herself. Knowing that this is the only hope.

However, he has unique plans. He looks at her just to let her know. Who is the boss now? He knows she would do anything for him. Asking her what she knows. He would let her go.

Lily knows that he is lying to her. She knows he just wants her to tell him all her secrets. Knowing that they used this on criminals. Just to get their top secrets. She knows that he is her mentor. Has deceived her and what she stood for.

This made her blood boil. Knowing what he could do with her. It also made her shiver with fear. He could kill her here. Then, her son and husband wouldn't know what had happened. She has a feeling. She needs to look around. To leave.

However, there is only one place to leave. It is through the door. He is in the doorway with a gun. Pointing at her. Getting ready to fire at her if she is to move.

Feeling betrayed while standing. Beside the chair. She is about to sit. Knowing the next thing. He would chain her with his handcuffs.

Even though she knows how to get out. She has taken a class to show her how. She knows that he doesn't know that. He knew everything that he taught her. Not the things she learned on her own. She couldn't use any of it on him. He will see it coming.

She will need to use the new things that she has learned. Out of the Army. Knowing that she will need to use it.

What she has learned. In the past few years. Not knowing that she would need it.

He continues to look at her. Just to let her know, to sit. Just so he can control her. Even better. Not knowing what she knows.

The more confusing he is. She is at peace.

Her Heavenly Father is giving her a gift. She knows that there will be a time for her to get out of this. Knowing that her prayers are being answered. Pushing forward in her faith. Knowing that she is to move to the spirit world. It would be his plan. Knowing she could see her daughter.

He looked at her and said, "Sit down." "You will not be getting away so fast." Looking up at the corner of the ceiling, I says, "I know all of your tricks; remember, I trained you." "I will kill you." With an eye roll to the ceiling. "I don't want to, but I will." "You are like a daughter to me, but they will kill my whole family." "If I don't stop you, they will stop me." Lily saw the eye rolling. "Then him." With a look of desperation. In his eyes. Knowing that he can't tell anyone what he is doing for the government.

She could see. He has to play a role. He didn't want to do this. She thought she knew him, but she didn't. Knowing that sound of desperation. Coming from his mouth. His eyes show it all. Wetness comes down to his jawline.

Her heart swells for him. Thinking that he is hard. Just like a stone. Finds out that he is human. He has emotions. She had never seen this before. Not from him.

With her hands cuffed to the chair. She scoots towards him. He backs up. With his gun pointed towards her. Lily did not know what he would do at that moment. Then remembering him looking towards the ceiling. Knowing they are watching him.

She looks at him. Trying to look into his eyes. Just to see that light. He used to have. Noticing his emotions is done. She could sense the fear in him. A storm is within himself. Lily doesn't understand it fully. The pain that he is living.

Trying her best to understand why? Would he work for evil men?

Understanding he wants to save his family. She needs to talk to him. Just to have him change his mind. Knowing that he needs to help save the innocent victims. His mind is on saving his family. Not understanding that he is deep undercover. Deeper than she knows. He was in thought.

Knowing there are more of these. To break them up. He thinks to himself. There are too many. I can't do this too many times. He knows that Lily isn't the only one. He knows that he won't make it through this time. Knowing that he needs to be right with his Heavenly Father. Having a feeling that his time is about up. Fighting all the way to live. He knows that he can't say a word to Lily.

Lily knows that she is thinking hard. By the actions on his face. They say it all.

He looks at Lily and asks her to forgive him. What he is going to do. He will sacrifice himself for his family. He is emotionally tired. There is too much evil in this world. Knowing that the Government needs his help. Looking at Lily with heartbreak.

Lily knows that look. A look of surrender. She saw this in Afghanistan. A brother gave up and came home in a coffin. Death is something they saw every day. Her heart goes out to him. Not knowing that the government put him here. He is a pawn in their game.

Knowing as she looks at him. She needs to get him out of there before he finds the girls.

Lily thinks to herself. She needs to talk to him. Just like he would do to her. When she felt like giving up.

She moves forward to him. Looks at him and tells him to stop feeling sorry for himself. You are better than this.

He looks at her. Making sure that she could see his eyes. Tells her to read his lips. This is much worse. Then what we went through in Afghanistan.

This is worldwide. Mothers and Father selling their children. Putting them in Hell. It never ends. You and I will not stop it. While waving his gun, and continues looking toward the ceiling. Again, she noticed. Lily keeps trying to remind him of his gun. She realizes that this isn't the same person she thought he was. This line of work isn't for everyone.

While he is going off. Lily could see a shadow. Knowing that they could come for her. By the way, he is talking to her. She thought they were coming for her and for him.

He noticed nothing around him. Still waving a gun. Not realizing the danger that will come to him.

Not knowing that the SWAT Team is nearby.

Lily is hoping and praying that Martha is safe and that she will get out. Thinking that this is it.

She will see her little girl soon. Knowing that her boy is going to need her. She needs to live.

He looks at her one more time. Knowing that he needs to realize what he is doing. Telling her I can't do this to you. Lily notices that there is a silencer. On the gun.

She looks at him. Knowing that he wants to die. He saw enough evil. Is ready to end it.

The shadow is coming closer. To where they are. They are just two rooms away. Know that they will be here in a few more steps. Lily's heart thumps to a new tune. Just knowing that in a few more steps. She could meet her Heavenly Father. Then, there were the innocent girls. Knowing they will go back. Not knowing who they are.

Wondering if they are evil men in white coats. As they come closer, she closes her eyes. Just to get ready for them.

Letting her mentor know that he should stop waving his gun. Just to let him know that they could be in danger. Trying her best to let him know quietly. That they could be in danger. Feeling that this will not end well. She knows that either. He or she could have the light leave his or her eyes. Or the other way. Her heart was sorrowful.

Looking at her mentor. Knowing by the way he is sitting. He would be the first one shot. She knows that she would have to be faster than them. Just to be safe from what comes out of the gun.

Knowing that they are coming. Her heart thumps to that familiar tune. She sits at the edge of the chair waiting for disaster to strike. Knowing that death will come soon. She feels it could be here.

Someone she doesn't know would rather kill Lily. Then someone she does.

She looks at him. With fear in her eyes. Knowing that he cares for her. He is going to have to make a choice.

He looks up and notices the shadows. His heart skips a beat. He knows that he needs to go. Before they would kill him. Not knowing who it is. Not knowing that the government needs him, he is deep undercover. To stop them. He also needs Lily to live. He had trusted her with his life before. However, he needs his family safe.

He looks at Lily and asks her. "Would you help me?"

Knowing that he needs to take these ropes off of her.

He knows that she won't stop. Until she sees the innocent safe.

Knowing that the shadow is coming closer. She closes her eyes. Hoping not to be seen. The shadow shoots her. Opening one eye. Just to see how close they are. Knowing that the first one to be shot would be him.

With his back towards the door. Trying quickly to free Lily.

CHAPTER 33

DEATH IS CALLING!

Meanwhile, Detective Binder quietly goes toward the end of the tunnel.

Letting undercover officers know they were ending with a wave of his hand.

Seeing rooms as he walks by. Let them know they are being watched. While the movement of the cameras. Going back and forth. Biner knew they were being watched. Let the men know to be ready for anything.

He has done this before. Feeling that he needs to check each room. Not knowing if he would have to. Take the light from humankind's eyes.

Thinking he was done. Doing this kind of job. This kind of life takes its toll on a person. He would know. His heart has become hardened. He was done with this. Now he knows. They need him once more. He thinks about all of this.

Passing each room. Wondering if he could save someone. The innocent need help. This town needs help. He knows what happens in these small towns.

He knows that the innocent will pay. They won't be safe. Young children for sale. Just to be used. Then when they are done.

They become trash. Never found and discarded. Knowing what he saw on the map. Their bodies will be ash.

As he comes closer to this door. He could hear someone breathing. Just as if someone is sleeping. Not knowing what is on the other side. It became very clear.

It could take the light from his eyes. Knowing that the enemy could be there. Wondering if this could be it. Knowing in this line of work. He had his gun ready to return fire first. Wondering if it could be a child.

Walking slowly, trying not to make a sound. Know that an evil man would not be sleeping on the job. Hoping that a child is the one.

Walking with caution. Into the doorway. Knowing that the sound got louder. He knew that it was a child by now. It sounded like a cry. Knowing if it was a cry for help.

Knowing what just happened. Looking around, trying to see. Without his google he couldn't see anything. Making sure he followed the sound of the innocent cry. Having one man, he gave him his goggles to see better.

Binder looked into a corner. Seeing the horror of the innocent. Knowing this evil person beaten him, then had his sick pleasure done. Then, left the little boy to go to his maker. Knowing that he could not say a word. All for a profit.

Bind blood boiled. He has been doing this for so long. It never changes. Knowing there is so much damage to the little boy. With these deep feeling, he might not make it. He is breathing shallow. His pause is faint. His eyes are losing their light. He has only a moment.

Binder bends down, leans him towards him. He hummed a song to him; he is a child of his father in heaven. With droplets coming down to his jawline. He is strong but not heartless.

Binder was going to stay until he took his last breath. Knowing that he couldn't save him. He has a son of this age.

Knowing he is going to tell these parents. He will never come back. Hoping that this child's pain will leave him soon. Binder's heart was showing through. After twenty years of fighting, they would become hardened.

Knowing time is standing still at this moment.

While there were no dry eyes among the men. They all knew what they were fighting for. Most of these men had children. Around the age of this boy. Knowing this needs to end, and out of their town.

While they all stood around. Knowing they were watching a life that was ending. Their hearts aced. This little boy had no chance of living. While they watched and prayed. They watched his last breath go out of him. Watching it floats towards the heavens. Knowing that he will never hurt again.

Binder continues for a few moments to sit there. Trying to get himself together. Realizing he can't stop it anymore. This evil will never end.

Binder called Terry to tell him what just happened. Capin needs to know where to pick up the body. Once the war is over. That another innocent child went home to his heavenly father.

Terry could hear it in his voice. This job he was done.

He needs to get up and move on. Time is ticking. He and the men need to move forward. Knowing there is more that needs to be saved. To push their heartbreak to the back of their minds.

Knowing that they are also being watched. These evil men will look for them.

While they move forward. Watching each step. Trying their best to be quiet enough not to give away their location. Knowing with every moment. They could lose their light in their eyes.

While they keep moving. Binder looked downward and noticed a red laser wire going from one end to the other of a doorframe. You couldn't see it if you didn't have goggles on.

They needed to go through one room to get to the other.

Binder used his hand to signal them to stop. He points downward. To let see what was waiting for them. They all know what they need to do to move to the next room. While they all step over.

Knowing they all know. What could have happened? They all know they must move forward. They keep going from room to room.

Knowing they have cleared rooms. They are still in danger.

Not to know how close they are.

Then they knew where the evil men were. People in white coats were bringing children into rooms.

Binder made a hand sign to stop.

Having these men stop meant their lives were in danger. Letting know they need to be watching what is happening. Giving them hand signals to record what was happening.

Seeing how they were branding them like cattle. Putting what Binder could see was tracking devices. The more they watched, the more they wanted to end it. Wondering how many there are.

While they are watching these people in white coats. Not paying any attention to what could happen.

One-man notices shadows and whispers. Knowing there could be an ambush. Move slowly to Binder. Letting him know there is somebody moving.

Knowing that he needs to go, he should check it out. This could start a fight that will be premature. They aren't ready yet. He wanted to get all the proof he could. These people killed this child or were involved somehow.

He knows that if he needed to, he would drop them quiet.

While he lets them know he will. Be checking these shadows and whispers.

Moving towards these shadows. Know this could be dangerous. Bring a few men with him. Noticing more white coats.

His sticky red liquid rushed through his veins. Knowing this isn't good. His men could lose the light from their eyes. He must protect them at all costs.

CHAPTER 34

SALVATION FOR THE GIRLS!

ily looks at him, saying to him, I understand why, but it is still wrong. Knowing the shadow is coming. She knew earlier she had seen people in white coats looking for her.

Knowing that her light in her eyes could be gone from him or them.

The first time since this whole thing happen her faith was wavering. Is her Heavenly Father going to help now?

Lily's mind goes back in time. Beginning to remember of time long ago. When Heavenly Father had her back. Knows she needs to believe he got this and all the children.

Lily felt powerful. Her father told her in her mind to get up. You got this. I will help you.

She stands up, looks at him. Knowing that he is not the leader anymore. She thought he was. He could take her life, but for now she is going to let him know. Either you help me or pay for it. She looks at him to let him know he could decide.

Remember, there were cameras around. Knowing his light from his eyes could become deemed.

Knowing that she needed to get out of there. She knows that the girls need to be safe as well.

These shadows are coming closer. They are on a mission to come and get her.

Having a feeling to stay and fight. Then, having a thought. She looks back at him. Just to let him. She needs to save these young girls.

While her veins are filling with red sticky liquid. There to remind her of danger is coming.

Walking over to this closet, and opened it. Bring out the two girls who are hiding. Still a little drugged from the poison they gave them.

Let him see what she was trying to save. Reminding him he could be a part of saving the innocent from evil. Knowing that he is deep with them. Can she save him? Once, he saved her so many times.

He looks at her, then the two girls. Told her, "I will lose my family." "They will kill my girl with the poison they gave these two girls." "They will kill my son, two." "My wife will be motherless." "I can't do this to her." "I can't let them kill these two angels either."

"I can't say too much; remember, we are being watched." As his eyes roll toward the other side of the wall.

Let Lily know danger was waiting for them. Knowing they need to go now.

Looking at Lily, "I know a way out." Lily looks at him. "How can I trust you?" "You were going to kill me." "You still could."

Looks at her to let her know, and the look said it all. He has so much sorrow about his family.

"I will go in front." "You follow me."

"That way, the girl will be safe." "When they are safe." "You and I will take care of this." "You will know the truth."

Lily could see his face. It said all she wanted to know. Understanding why, how could his family? Be safe.

At this moment, her feelings need to be on hold. These girls need to be safe.

They are coming for her. Time to move. Lily looks on while he moves. Leading the way. Lily doesn't know. Where they are going. Knowing that anything could happen. She knows she could see them.

While he leads them from room to room. Wondering did these rooms had a camera in them also?

With each room they got to where they weren't so drugged up. Lily could feel they was so scared though. Knowing this feeling she has within her. She needs to duck. Knowing this could be a feeling of doom. She needs to stop and hide.

In a few seconds, it happens. In a moment she hears a loud popping sound. Know what it was.

Seeing him holding his shoulder. Sliding downward to the floor. Seeing red sticky liquid running down his arm.

Knowing what just happened. This is first-aid time. She rips his sleeve off. Ties it to his arm. She knew she had to stop the red sticky liquid coming out of his body.

She could see these girls' looks of horror. Knowing this was going to be something they wouldn't forget.

Knowing there is no time to wait. Their lives are in danger. Lily grabs the girl and shoves them under a desk.

Hoping they stay there. Told them to stay there, she needed to help the man that was shot.

Knowing they were panicky, because she was. Trying her best to calm them. Her heart went out to them. Being put in this world. Lily's emotions showed. Knowing she needs to swallow her lump. If she is going to make it through this. She needs to hide deep down within herself.

She needs to get him. Knowing they will come for him. She has to save him. No time to waste, he needs her. She isn't he.

Wondering would he really, have killed her. Her heart keeps reminding her of the danger they are in.

While she comes to the doorway. Thinking that she needs to have her gun ready to go.

Knowing that she could take the light out of a human being. Being here is taking its toll on her.

Seeing shadows coming towards him, she needs to get him now.

Her heart is beating to a fast tune. Warning her to hurry, time is running away from her.

Being thankful that he isn't too far from the doorway.

She takes a few steps towards him, pop-pop.

Knowing they are in danger, the girls. How to get them out of here. He looks Lily in the eye. "They want them."

"They won't stop." "Their lives and you are in danger."

"We need to get you out and NOW." Lily looks at him. "You mean." "You are in." "Yes, I am."

Leaning toward her, "I am what you call undercover."

With a whisper, so the cameras. Could hear him.

As he tried to stand up. He checks his arm, noticing the bullet went through. Knowing that the bleeding hasn't stopped yet. However, he could use his hand to shoot.

Looking at Lily with a go-get-them look. Let's try this again. This time. I will let you be the leader. I am so sure you would be quicker than I was. Now let's make sure you take off the safety. Lily looks at her gun, and sure enough it was there.

Moving through the room they were in. Making sure it was safe. Trying not to be seen. While they move from room to room. Leaving red stick liquid behind them.

They could hear hearts beating to the tune of fear. The last room. Now they are out in the open. Lily gun and loaded it, ready to take the light from someone's eyes.

She could feel every thump. Reminding her. Her veins are gorging themselves. With her red sticky liquid.

Knowing she has so much at stake. Wondering what is happening with Martha.

Not paying attention on this mission she is on now. She knows she needs to come back on this mission.

Looking back at him. Noticing he didn't look good. Looking and seeing his blood. Following him. Droplets add up. Also, noticing he is stumbling. Walking toward his way.

He looks into her eyes. Spoke to her. "They hit me in two places, one a major artery."

"It won't stop." "You know what will happen." "It will bleed out." "Just leave me here." "Please promise me to get my daughter." "The boss has her." "Getting me to work for him." "Knowing that she is in danger as well." "They will poison her." "Then she will have her soul leave her body."

Lily remembers Sam's cousin says that his daughter. Had her light taken from her. While they were whispering to each other.

Shadows are showing again. Knowing she needs to help him. Get to a safe spot.

Knowing she must get the girl. Knowing they are farther up. Know that this could go all wrong.

Her heart beat that tune of dome. Once more.

Wanting to quickly before they would find her. Lily knows she is in the open.

The shadows are coming closer. Hoping not to be noticed. Telling the girl to hurry. Knowing they must get somewhere safe. Hoping they wouldn't be seen.

CHAPTER 35

SHADOW OF DEATH!

Sam takes a deep breath for a moment. Knowing he was so close to being in the spirit world.

Running towards Martha, knowing she was safe. Knowing how this could have gone the opposite.

Looking at all of rows and rows of children. Wondering how they are going to save them all? Shaking his head.

Knowing that some of them. Already look as if their light from their eyes has left.

Being a military man. He knows they need more men. Not knowing that the Swat team was coming.

Looking at these rows of children, having lost emotions. Not knowing where to start. Too many. Too much heartbreak.

Knowing men like this. Need to be out of this world, gone. Knowing this sickness, is it over the world?

Sam looks at these innocent children.

Looking at each cage, he sees a child of heavenly father. These people have no right to cage these little souls.

While he was trying to understand why they did this.

Cameras are watching. To show the evil people. Where the rescuers are. The evil is in protecting their profit or their bottom line.

Not knowing there is a minor war. Coming their way. To take their souls from them.

While Sam is trying his best to figure out how to do this.

Undercover cop saw some shadows. Wondering where they are coming from.

Sam wasn't paying any attention. He was trying to keep it together. His red stick liquid would boil. With each cage he would see. It was taking everything he had not to take their lives from them.

In every cage, the child has had some poison to shush them. Not known by looking at them. If their souls were even there. Wanting to save them all.

Knowing that some of these kids. Their parents are looking for them. Then some have. From the one that loves them.

Knowing that some of these kids will go to the state. Not to have loved one's waiting for them. His heart aches for them. They have no chance of knowing love without pain.

While he goes to each cage. With his heart tumbling with each cage, is trying to see if they wake up. Wanted to know what he could do.

Seeing that some were not coherent. Hoping that all will come out of this hell.

Noticing some not moving. They didn't even look as if they had a breath of life in them.

He didn't have the keys, though he wanted to go in there to save them.

Standing at the cage with droplets rolling down his cheeks and hitting his shoes. Grabs the bars. With a righteous anger. Scream out quietly.

Wondering if they've made it to their father in heaven. Knowing they will pay someday, but when? How long does the innocent pay for evil men?

CHAPTER 36

GIVING LIFE TO THE INNOCENT!

eanwhile, the undercover cop. Keep seeing shadows, wondering what they could be. Something didn't seem right. Having this feeling of doom.

Knowing she needs to check it out. Taking a few men with her. A small group.

While they head out. She took her piece out, and so did they as well. Ready to take the evil light away.

Knowing that evil is here. Knowing that light could emanate from their eyes.

While she follows the shadow. At a slow pace. Using her hand to lead. Not knowing what lay ahead of them.

Knowing that a war will break out. She points toward the men. Waving them toward herself. Knowing that she will have to take them with her.

While she goes toward the shadow. Slowly and steadily, she steps. Knowing this could go badly.

Having a few following her. With each step, her heart sings that old tune of doom.

Following this shadow. Knowing that if it knew. Her soul would leave her body. Even might get her brothers.

Wondering would they would even be ready for it? War is here.

All these children need to be saved.

With each step, there is a reality of what could happen.

Knowing that she is in a den of evil. Having her men stop and hide. They are coming for them. Wanting them out of sight.

Knowing she is coming to the end of the tunnel. The men came to a stop with the wave of her hand.

They were being watched, and they didn't know. While she looks up. What she saw was doom.

Seeing a black round camera recording every move. She knew there could be a surprise attack. They will not be ready.

Knowing these distinguished men could have the light taken from their eyes.

They all knew war was coming for them.

Knowing that now is the time, they need to act. Deep down they know they are coming for them.

Getting into position for the war to come down on them. Knowing they need more men for this war.

Not knowing that the Swat team is a few tunnels away.

While their hearts beat to the tune of doom. Knowing this war could be their last.

Being trained for this was their job.

She looks at these twenty - year - olds. First time for him to be put into a war. She sees him having an earthquake within himself.

Being taught by his mother. How to pray. While his gun is doing the shakes, he is praying. To see his family again. Just to tell them he loves them.

Knowing this is his first and last mission. Praying for it to be different.

With the enemy on their way. Let them know to be ready. They are coming. War is here.

Knowing they were to lose, the children will pay for their innocence.

They will move forward towards evil, even if light leaves their eyes.

As they blinked, it started. War is here. Firing on both sides. Men fall on both sides.

The undercover cop saw a metal garbage bin and threw herself into it. Her brain was telling her about the pain in her thigh. Red stick liquid coming down her leg. There to tell her of what just happened.

Peeking under the lid. Just having a few inches. In recording all that was happening. Knowing that this would be evidence.

She was trying not to move or even say a word. Knowing that they will take her, for a profit or have her light leave her eyes.

Watching each one fall. Knowing what she is seeing and recording. If they knew where she was. No one would know her story. Knowing these men was out in the open.

Watching them walk towards the twenty-year-old, not caring. How young he is. He looked him in the eyes and said, "You will meet your maker today." The twenty-year-old looked the evil man in the eyes. I will meet my God today.

While the evil man heard this, he became wroth. Then, put a hole between his eyes of the twenty-year-old. No more sound came out of him.

The undercover cop becomes emotional. Swallowing it down. Trying her best not to make a sound. Her heart was pounding so hard. Knowing that, she needs to calm herself. Knowing she couldn't do anything about it

She recorded each soul drop. Hoping they don't find here. Knowing she needs to hide this evidence.

Evil men go back to see if they got rid of the enemy. Watching the video. From the beginning of the war, they just had.

They saw it; one got away. They know she can't run. It looked as if she got wounded.

Undercover cop knows that if she doesn't get help soon. She could lose all of her red-stick liquid.

Then, her soul would leave her body. She would be with her brothers in arms.

Knowing she had to tie something around her thigh now before it was too late, but what? Noticing a piece of cloth. She is lying on it. Knowing she needs to move to get off of it.

While she is trying to tie it, she does not know how long it is. Going to last. Hoping that she makes it.

Wounding about her family. Her two-year-old could be without a mother, and her husband. Could be a widower.

She feels she needs to check her phone and send a text to her daughter and husband. Making sure no sound comes out.

Wondering if it showed all the damage. That these evil men have done.

Her blood wants to boil, but her emotions need to be down. At this moment.

They know where she is. Knowing they will come for her.

She could hear them. Her mind is letting her know. It is getting close for her. What is she going to choose? It might not be what she gets.

She could hear them coming, and they're coming for her. While they open the garbage bin lid. Noticing her beauty.

Knowing that they need to stop her red sticky liquid. Then they will do with what they want.

It is up to the boss man. Knowing that the boss man will want her for a good profit.

While they were taking her out of the garbage bin. She turns to the gray world.

The last thought was. "I will become their prize." Knowing the story won't be told for now. However, someone will find her phone someday. The truth will come out.

CHAPTER 37

PAYMENT OF EVIL FOR DEATH!

Sam needs to rest. He knows he needs to watch how far he pushes himself. His brain let him know grayness is coming for him again. The more he pushes, the faster it comes.

Knowing that Martha needs to sit beside him. He wants to make sure she is safe.

He sits down with one eye open. Taking deep breaths. Hoping it will help.

Thinking and talking to himself. Wondering, this is too easy. Evil doesn't end this easily.

Knowing something is so wrong. His heart is beating to the tune of doom. Knowing this will not end well.

Telling the men to be ready for anything. They have been on high alert. Having a feeling of doom as well.

The action of a military man is to be ready for anything.

Sam's body goes toward the gray world. Knowing this is a good time for the enemy to hit.

Hoping and praying as the grayness his. Sliding down from the chair and onto the floor.

Fading into another world. Begged to go back. Fighting with everything he has in him. His goal is to save his daughter.

Wondering how to get back know. Trying his best to do anything. He knows he needs to get back into danger. They all could be in.

Of the few SWAT team men that were left behind, they watched over the children.

Not knowing what was in store. They watch over Martha and Sam. While one sat there to make sure he would too soon. Talking to Martha. She felt safe.

Wondering where the others are. Knowing there were more. What happens to them?

The SWAT team had only a few men. There weren't enough human resources for a war.

Hearing a screaming sound. Coming from the tunnels. She knows evil will come for her.

While these brave men run toward the sounds. This is the sound of evil all around her. While her father was out of it, not hear a sound.

Martha hears her safety being shattered. She sits as if she is a statue, watching men fall. Watching their light leave their bodies.

They have come back to claim what they have taken for themselves.

These innocent children are theirs. They took them and did the work. To make sure they could profit from their innocence.

One of the evil men notices Martha sitting beside a man on the floor.

She knows at this moment. Her father couldn't save her. She was trying to act as if they weren't there. Not understanding, they were there to claim her.

She would be a prize to get profit from. While acting as if she can't see them, she knows they will take her. Taking her from her father.

Willing to give her poison just to get her where they want her.

Martha looks upward toward these two men. Holding her by the arms. While another man holds her head toward the camera. The boss.

While he stands there, Sam's cousin. Walks over and stands there beside him.

Martha's heart sank, with in herself. To know they are working together.

Sam's gray world is lifting. He knows that the way he left isn't the same.

Noticing that Martha isn't there. Sitting upward. Looking upward, saw a man there. Sam asked in a whisper-like voice. Trying to get his marbles together.

Sam's cousin knew his boss loved to trap parents. Help him with his business. By threatening to poison their children until he gets what he wants.

Their light dimmed in their eyes. He sees that he is a monster. Knowing his day will come.

This boss man wanted Sam to be forced to work with him. Let him know that danger will come to his last child.

Sitting him upward, just to sit him in the chair he sat before. Chaining him as you would an animal.

Meanwhile, Martha screamed, "Please don't hurt me." "Leave me alone." "Daddy, don't do it." "They take my soul, anyway."

This boss looked at her and then at the men who held her. He gave them an evil grin. They knew what that meant. He will do what he wants to do to her. They all know what that is.

He looks at Sam. You see, I have the card; you have nothing. I will tell you what to do.

You see, you have what I want. I need you. To make an account for over sea. I need to have the business. Get started in selling young boys for labor and young girls for men drives.

You see, a person's soul means nothing to me. Take the innocent and play with them. Then, take their light from them. It matters not to me.

So, you see, your daughter will be gone unless you help me.

Sam looks at him. "What do I do?" "Please don't hurt my daughter."

Know how the army trained them to act and work with the enemy. Work their own tricks on them. The games begin.

Sam knows this will be hard on Martha, but in order for them to get out of this.

Let the boss know that he needs to have the chains taken off.

He needs to make a phone call. Undoing these chains. He falls to the floor. Knowing he is weak. Martha broke free for a moment. Runs toward her father. Tries to help him before they get the chance to grab her again. Grabbing her so hard. It left her arm black and blue.

While she was screaming, "Daddy, save me." While they were carrying her away. Sam looks at his daughter until his red sticky liquid boils. Knowing there isn't anything he could do.

Sam prays for mercy. Knowing that he would love at that moment... to put a hole in his chest. Evil must be gone.

As they take Martha to the boss's office. Knowing he will take advantage of her. He loves weak people. It has a way of making him feel big.

As he leaves Sam's cousin in charge. He turns around to let Sam know that his daughter will please him soon.

CHAPTER 38

GOING BACK INTO THE LOIN DEN!

Lily knows she needs to find a way out. Knowing that her mentor needs medical treatment. And the girls need their freedom.

Her mind is aching at this moment. Wondering how she is going to do this.

While her mentor is leaving a trail of his red sticky liquid. Knowing that soon he could lose his light from his eyes soon.

Knowing she needs to get out. Wondering how? Asking her mentor if he knew of a way out, for them.

With a look of shame. "I know how, but we need to hurry."

"They are coming." "They will take the girls back." "Then they will have my soul leave my body." "Then they will." "Take the light out of my daughter, eyes." "After they take your fist."

Lily looks at him. "Well then, we need to go NOW." She helps him up. Then lean him up against the tunnel wall.

Knowing she needs to get the girls. Knowing that they need to know to be quiet. That if they want the evil men to know where they are. They need to be quiet.

Letting know not to say a word.

They move forward with a mission to get out to safety.

Knowing the evil men are looking for them.

Knowing their goal is to destroy innocents.

Lily knows that her mentor needs help. She leans him against her. Then move forward. Have the girls follow her. From behind, knowing it would be safer for them.

Coming toward two tunnels. Look at her mentor asks him, "Which one do we take?" He pointed to the right. They move forward.

Stopping to check if they followed. Leaning him against the wall. Takes out her binoculars.

Checking up ahead to see if they were being watched. Knowing it is a chance. If there were any, they would be in places you couldn't see.

She looks carefully, checking more than once. Only found one.

Knowing how to become a ghost. With her heart beating to a tune. With her veins becoming engorged. While her body is letting her know.

There is still a risk. For freedom to happen.

Her mentor and these girls need to live.

Knowing at this moment, she needs to see this through. Then she will go back for Martha.

Let the mentor know, "We need to hug the wall." Letting the girls know how to walk as ghosts. While they walk past.

Knowing they passed that test, with plenty more to come.

While she keeps stopping at moments to check. Knowing it could change within seconds.

Lily prayed with every step she took. Trying to have the faith to turn to hope and to have a miracle.

As the girls became more frightened with every step they make. That they make towards freedom. Within their fear, it was coming out in noise.

Lily got tier of it. She turned around and said with a look they knew. "I am trying to get you out of here." "To your family, so shut up." "You are going to let them know we are, so shut up."

Lily is wearing down under the load she has. Know she has to save everyone. Knowing what the lord would want her to do. She must keep going. As she keeps praying, she moves forward.

With each step, she thinks of Martha. Wondering was she bought. Even worse, did her soul leave her body yet? Wondering what happened to her.

She keeps praying as she walks. Once her job is done. She will be back to save Martha.

Her faith is going back and forth. Asking her father in heaven for forgiveness, she had doubts. She had become weak. asked Heavenly Father, "Are you listening to," "Do you hear me?" Hearing a voice in her brain. "I am here."

Just as she wonders. With frustration, she sees light.

Getting her binoculars. Looking ahead. Her heart leaps with joy. Still, they know they are in danger. At the end of the tunnel. There in the corner. Looking both ways.

Lily's heart had become sorrow. She knows it is going to take a miracle. How are they going to get bye?

While she stops to figure out how they are going to get out. Without them knowing.

Walking near the wall. Just to be safe. Praying while walking back and forth. Her mentor knew that look. Letting her know that she could go behind the video camera. Hugging the rock. It wouldn't be able to see us.

While Lily looks him in the eyes, knew he has little time left. She needs to get him help now.

Then she was told in her mind, go now. As she grabs her mentor. Let the girl know to do what she does. They move forward.

Getting closer to the light. Knowing each step will bring them to freedom.

Then Lily whispered to the girl to stop. She needs to let them know how to slip through. While her stomach told on her. Ready to have nothing come up.

Knowing the danger of their seeing them. This would be bad for them.

Her mind goes to her husband. Wondering if the last kiss would be their last. And the hugs she gave her children. Wondering would be her last. Hoping for many more.

While she keeps trying her best. Having her droplets falling onto her cheeks.

Knowing she cannot stop evil no matter what she does. Knowing that her children have to grow on this earth.

Lily wanted to go back to this task. Knowing that her mentor was failing.

They have come to the end of the tunnel. Knowing it is time to go. Looking at the girls, I know it's time to go.

While she goes to save them all. He told her in a whisper, "Please save my daughter." "He will poison her." "The boss needs to be stopped." "Please stop him." "He will not stop using parent." "They will do anything to save their child." "He needs a hole between his eyes."

"He looks for people who are high in their business." "There is a new name on his list." "His name is Sam. "He is a banker. *Lily knows by now. Sam is in danger as well.*

"I am so sorry he found me." "My daughter is in there." "Find her and save her." "Let her know that I love her." "Let her know that I am so sorry."

He looks at her to let her know. He didn't plan this.

While he gave his confession. They are on the field. She knows her prayers. Just turned into a miracle. Knowing that she needed to put out her piece.

Thinking to herself, this is only a six-shooter. If a war were to break out there, they would be gone.

Lily looks around. It was time to rest. Knowing the building was just a few steps away. They could hide there. Just for a few moments.

Wondering if Terry was where she left him. Hoping to get back to him in one safe piece.

After waiting a few moments, she headed back towards the truck. Hoping she gets there in time to get her mentor the medical help he needs.

She could feel a light pulse. Knowing he has lost a lot of red sticky liquid. He will need to get more to save him.

Knowing this crowd will tell on her. These people who are blanketing the sidewalks. Will do anything to get their fix. Even if it is the innocent.

Lily keeps trying to get the girl to walk faster. Their little bodies are done. These little girls were around the ages of six or seven.

Walking around the crowds, having to walk beside her. Let them know if they don't keep up; they could be back in the evil people's hands.

Knowing with each second of time. Her heart lets her know she is still alive. Her stomach is letting her know it is there.

She looks around. Noticing the area. She didn't have to look far. Her heart leaps for joy.

Noticing that the undercover cops are there. Yell in their direction. Terry notices who it was. Dashing toward her way. Wanting to hold her, not letting go. He couldn't, she is holding a male up.

Noticing two little girls coming out from behind her.

Lily gives a grin to Terry. Gives a wink, as she always did. Just to let him know she loves him.

As the Chief walks over to talk to Lily. He notices that the person she brought back with her need's medical treatment.

Lily looks at him. He is an army officer. Shot in the line of duty. Once in the arm and in the though. He has lost a lot of red sticky liquid. He will need more.

Looking at him, and lets him know. He will get the help he needs. The other thing about your daughter will be done. With a wink.

Knowing that he is safe. She needs to save other children.

Knowing how bad it is. She needs to do something about it.

She looks at Terry; "We need to talk." He knows what this means.

He looked at her and told her, "I don't want you to go back." She looks at him. "Honey, you know I have too."

"This whole thing has a twist to it." "Sam and Martha are in a game they will not win." "They both will lose." "Can't say too much. Because I don't know that much yet."

Looking at him, "I know that you want to help, right" "You see, baby," I said, "I do too." She looks at him, with wetness in her eyes. Letting him know. This time she might not come back; this is war.

She needs to be ready to go. With one last touch. Looks at Terry said. "Pray for us to make it out alive."

Letting him know that she has evidence on her phone.

She needs the right equipment, as the SWAT team does. She let them know that some tunnels need to go. The SWAT team needs to know. They will need to know which one. There are many that lead down to the mine.

Looks at Terry, "You know how to read these maps." "Bring me home to you." "I need to hear you." "I will see everything with theses googles."

She leans over. Her heart thumb to his touch. While she leans into him. Knowing and hoping this isn't the last time. Looking downward with wetness in her eyes.

Torn between doing the right thing and wanting to stay. She needs to do this. No one else can save Martha.

While Lily looks at Terry. Letting him know. "I need to save Martha." "I am the only one who can."

Terry looks at Lily. "You don't know." "Sam is in there." Lily's eyes wide open, "What?"

"I need to get in there NOW."

With one last look back. Told him, "Bring me home."

Knowing she must push forward. While her heart stayed back. With her love.

Looking toward her love's way. Knowing that this war could end it all. War is here to claim the innocent.

Turning her head to move forward. She knows that she is right. With her savior.

Knowing what all this will do to her family. Therefore, she quit before. Not thinking she would be drug back into this evil world.

Knowing as she gets closer to the tunnel. Her heart beat to the tune of doom. Once more. Knowing she is entering evil.

This time she is a little wiser. The evil she has seen. Knowing what they will do. Seeing the layout. Knowing where the children are.

The white coats were on the lookout for her. Knowing that she was their enemy.

As she enters the black tunnel. Hugging the wall as before. Her heart tries to skip thumps. Her heart was letting her know danger ahead. Noticing sound ahead of her.

Leaning up against the tunnel wall. Let Terry know that there are whispers. Wanting to know if the SWAT team was in the tunnel ahead of her.

Wondering if she should get ready. To take the light out of someone's eyes. With each step she takes. Her heart beat to the tune of doom. Having an earthquake within herself.

Knowing at any moment. Her soul could leave her body.

Waiting for Terry to answer back. "Yes, Lily."

"They are in the next tunnel over." "You need to head over that way."

Lily understood what she needed to do. However, still a little cautious. Making sure her hand is on her piece. Ready to guard herself. In position, and ready just in case. She would run into the white coats.

Knowing that it was so odd. It was too easy to get back in. "Why?"

Her mind thinks like an evil person. Wondering and looking around. The tunnels were big enough to pull a truck through. Enough to haul things.

Noticing that these could be a way for the evil people. To leave their town. With their profit. Start somewhere else.

Lily knows the first thing. She needs to do. Letting Terry know. The tunnel she is in. Is enormous.

This is the place they plan on moving their sexual and labor slaves. If they are going to stop them. They shut off their escape.

While she is talking to Terry. She could hear voices coming closer. Letting him know she needs to go. Just in case the white coats show up. Praying just in case.

Making sure her piece would be quiet. When she would use it. Just so the sound wouldn't draw attention to her. Knowing that it would tell on her.

Knowing this could go badly for her. Standing still to be ready. Being out in the open. Knowing that this could be where they take light from her eyes.

While her heart is telling on her with each thump. Gorging her veins with red sticky liquid. To remind her. She is still alive.

Knowing that her body was letting her know the old familiar feeling. Therefore, she didn't want to do this anymore. She is here to save Martha. Then she will be done.

As she keeps watching, she sees a shadow lurking cautiously. Wondering who it is. Looking to see if they wear a white coat.

Waiting for them to come around the bin. Holding her breath. This is it.

Her hands are on her piece. Ready just in case. Those men in white coats. Come for her. Her back was against the wall. Hoping to hide from the enemy.

Her heart tells on her. While the shadows come for her. Closer and closer they come. Watching with her night goggles. Knowing this will tell on them.

By the sound of the footsteps. They came through the right tunnel. By the sound of footsteps. There was more than one.

The closer they get. The tighter she hugs the wall. Noticing a small hole in the wall.

They are upon her. She could feel every heartbeat in her body. Her breathing became shallow. Not wanting to be noticed.

People in white coats are looking for Lily. Seeing her on the camera. Knowing she was there.

No surprise attack. On these white coats today.

Knowing she needs to slip out of there. Take herself out of danger.

Walks out of the area quickly and quietly. While they see her on the camera. Sending the white coats after her.

Knowing she was in trouble. She could have a couple. Leave their souls but not all of them.

Letting Terry know that they were after her. If she doesn't make it. She was sorry, and she loved him.

He let her know that if she could hold out. The SWAT team was on its way. "Just hold on, dear, PLEASE."

Terry knows this is not good, and his heart lets him know. Praying within himself.

Trying to have the faith of a mustard seed. But oh, how it is wavering at this moment.

Lily tries to find a place to hide. Looking in the tunnel rock. Noticing a black round camera mounted in the rock.

She knew that they knew. She went out and then came back in. They knew about the girls and her mentor.

Now she knows that her mentor's daughter is in danger. Now she is really begging to see so many kids need to be saved.

Wondering how many will become angels. Knowing one is too many.

Her heart aches for the mothers who lose their children. This hole will stay empty. Knowing this feeling herself.

Knowing that she needed to get out of this terrible spot she was in. Her enemy was close by. Knowing she could lose everything.

She sees a spot. A crack in the wall. This was a perfect spot. Knowing this, the to hide.

Watching them walk by. Noticing that these men were giants. Knowing that she would never have had a chance. They would have had her do what they wanted.

As they walk by, looking to end her. Her heart tells her by sending her. Thumped to the tune of the dome she was in.

Trying not to breathe hard. Knowing that it would take one deep breath for them to know where she was. This crack was hiding her from danger. From a distance.

Then she saw men drop. Watching their souls leave their bodies. Lily's heart ached for them. They lost their souls to evil.

This wonderful SWAT team came in at the right time. Lily was very thankful. Knowing that this could have gone a different way. Thanking heavenly father. She knew who was in charge.

Thanked the SWAT team for showing up when they did. Wondering how they got there so fast.

Hello, "I'm the captain of this team." "We have been told to come and rescue." "Someone who was Lily." "Is that you?"

Lily looks at them all. "Yes, that is me."

Captain looked back and said, "Good, let's go get the victims." "Save them from these evil monsters."

BEGINNING OF A RESCUE!

inder knows they need to stop these men in white coats. Knows this is the time to end all this evil.

As he looks at the men. He told them, "This needs to stop now." "Who is with me?"

Knowing how they all look at each other. With their hearts broken, of what they just experienced.

While they all looked at Captain Binder. Letting him know. These evil men. Needs to be stopped at all costs. There light from their eyes needs to be taken.

They all agreed to end this. This requires silence. Knowing what he meant by that. They need to be quick in what they do.

Knowing their jobs. This is also personal. Seeing the damage.

Following these dark shallows. Knowing that they need to drop them now. If the shadow knew they were being followed. They would call in their men.

Binder doesn't have enough men to have a shootout with the enemy.

Knowing that he needs to get back to the other men. There is a greater danger there.

With each step reminded them of the danger they were in. Knowing that at any time. It could hit.

Binder telling them what to do with hands. Making sure they understood. What would be done?

Keeping silent between them, they knew if there was one screw up it could end it. Their hearts were telling on them.

Then, one-man trips over a stone. That was enough to get the attention of the evil men.

Binder knew that swiftness had to happen, NOW. Taking their pieces out. No sound came, men dropping. Knowing one still had his light in his eyes.

Noticing he was a young man. Having a hole in his leg. An earthquake was within him. Fear had become a part of him. Fear shone through the light in his eyes.

Knowing he wasn't American. They couldn't understand him. Thinking that was evil. Not known, he once had a home, with family.

Binder knew this was a boy, not a man. This male body was telling on him. His actions spoke the truth. Knowing this teen taken for a shield. He was replaceable.

Binder red, sticky liquid, boiled. Although for years he tried to stop this. It has done nothing.

Knowing this will be his last. He done with this kind of life.

He needs to come back to his job now.

Knowing that the bodies need to be moved.

Not letting the evil people know. They are there.

Hiding these bodies and moving on. They will pick them up later. Gathering their stuff to move on.

Looks at the young man. Shows him they will help him. To move forward. Knowing he was also a victim.

Having so much taken from the innocent.

Moving through the tunnels. Using his hand. To guide them. Hearing whispers near them. Knowing they are back in danger.

Looking at his men. Letting them know. Danger was back to claim them.

Walking towards the quiet sounds. A feeling of doom was coming back to them. Knowing they are coming back to claim. What was theirs?

They are coming closer. The team gets ready with their pieces. Knowing this could go so wrong.

Binder goes ahead; his piece was up and ready. To have someone's soul leave the body.

He takes a deep breath. To remind him, what he hates about this job.

Then, his earpiece worked to remind him. Terry was warning him that another team was coming in to help. One of them was his wife. Her name was Lily. Be on the lookout. They're coming your way.

He lets Terry know with a thankful heart. His heart beat back in tune, calm.

Binder takes his piece and releases the hammer. Still being cautious. Knowing this could still go wrong.

Waiting to see if they were coming. Knowing he would need their help. To triumph in this war.

While they were waiting for this team to show up. They made their way back toward where they had come from.

Knowing that they need to have control over that room. Where the victims were. Binder knows if they could take over that room. They could see over everything and win this war.

Taking one step at a time. Watching the team save the day. Wondering where they were. They were in a war, with no time to waste.

Then quietly they showed up. Binder walks over toward Lily. Told her in a whisper. "You must be Lily." "Terry told me you would show up."

"Your team and mine need to have a briefing." "Something has come up." "Your team needs to know this." Lily looks at him. "Okay, where do you want to go?" Binder looks at the floor. "Here is good."

As Binder talks about the plan of taking over the control room. What they were going to do and how. Looking at both teams, that became one in action. Know they are ready to fight.

Getting up and moving as a team. One for all. Is what they believe. Ready to fight with their brother.

Moving through the tunnels. Step by step, they work to save the innocent.

Their hearts were to save the children. Knowing that they might not save all.

Lily's mind goes toward Martha. With her heart aching for her. Knowing that this could go all wrong.

While she followed Binder, she was being led to a place she didn't know. With each step, wondered when she could save Martha and go home.

Her heart reminds her where she was. Still in danger around every corner. Knowing that they could still be on their video.

She knows she must move forward. Her heart was back with Terry. Hoping she can make it back to him. Knowing this could go so wrong.

These men on this team think back to their families. Knowing their light could leave their eyes this time. There will be a hole in their family.

Knowing this was a large team. Lily wondered when they would break off.

Wondering about stepping through these tunnels. Her heart is beating to the tune of doom once more. She knew this was a warning.

Whispering to Binder to let him know that they could be watching them. He looks at her to let her know. There was a control room. They will battle for it.

While he looks at her, he tells her that the victims were in there.

Lily tells him that there was an enormous room of cages of victims. Binder looks at her. With a look of heartbreak. It doesn't end.

Telling Lily there are too many high-up people involved. With this. It's not just about sex. They also sell these victims for labor.

These evil men and women sell these precious children of our Heavenly Father. It never ends for them.

Binder gives the hand sign to stop. Lily knew that by his look. It was about to become a war.

Binder points towards the tunnel downward. She could see a room. This could go so wrong.

She and Binder went forward. Making sure they had become quite as church mice. Having her heart with each step tell on her.

Binder waved his hand to follow. Just for backup. Know he will need it. Not knowing for sure how many evil men. They will have to fight.

Binder looked at Lily to tell her that if they can get into the control room. They could leave a team in the room watching.

While another goes and gets the victims out. Then, they get the monsters and make them pay for what they had done.

Binder looks at Lily; they both knew it was time. Let the team know they need to start. They are taking this room.

With no sound of war. It came as a surprise. People coming and going. It came to a stop. Men fell with their souls leaving their bodies.

Then Binder found that a few men had holes. Needed to stop their red sticky liquid to stop.

He takes his shirt off, tears it into sheets. Asks the men to mean the men who's wounded.

Binder goes into the control room. Looked at the screen. It told every move that was being made.

He calls out to Lily. She was helping the men with wrapping wounds.

She walks in, notices a child in the corner with a gun. Binder didn't even notice.

Lily stops, gets down to the floor, from a distance. Talking to the child. Trying to calm him down. Let's him know that it was okay to feel frightened. That she was too.

Looking at him, asking him to hand the gun to her. She wanted to feel safe, but she could not. With him having a gun.

Binder watched Lily as she worked her magic. With this child. The child wasn't frightened of her. He was talking to her.

Binder looked at the screen again. Seen bodies. It looked as if their souls had left their bodies. Calls Lily over to see. While she looks at the screen.

She sees Sam tied up and they have Martha. They were leaving.

Leaving Sam with some other men. This means danger for Sam. Knowing that Martha was in trouble of leaving the country. Knowing that the boss man has her.

She knew that this boss tries the good first before he shares for a profit.

Knowing that she needs to go to find Martha and Sam. She knows she can't save both.

Knowing she needs to ask Binder for help to save Sam. Looking at him, she asked.

Knowing that they need to hurry if they are going to save the day. Knowing that this team was big enough to break into two groups.

Let Terry know that they will be doing a rescue. They are going to need more men NOW. Get them from other states if you need to.

Terry not knowing how to do that. He has never done that before. Knowing he has a few men, that was over the state line. They have done this before.

Wondering whether they would do this. They were good old boys. They had no problem in aiming at the evil. He knew that he must call them now.

He has called them to let them know what was happening in their small town. Terry let Binder know that he has some more men coming. These men would take a life first and then ask questions later.

Lily and Binder looked at each other and got their teams ready to go. They knew that time was ticking. Lives are at stake here.

Must go now. Looking at the few men they were going to leave behind. Let them know, to let them know where they are going. Letting them know more men will come in to help.

CHAPTER 40

NEED A MIRACLE!

Lily knew she could see her soul leave her body or Martha's. Knowing most of the time her faith was strong. Now she doesn't know.

She knows most people don't make it out. Praying that she could get her out of this world. This evil world. Knowing that it will take the hand of God. To get out of this mess.

Moving forward with each step telling her. Her life was in danger. Her heart was beating to a tune. Letting her know — for now she was alive.

Wondering was Martha. Knowing she was with an evil man, but who? This was a question. Knowing that she has never seen him before.

Knows she doesn't know all the bad guys. In the line of work, she was doing.

Therefore, she doesn't do it anymore. There were eviler guys than good guys.

Trying to put her mind back on track. Knowing the men were there to help. Knowing them all. Could walk with the ghosts soon.

She also knew that the men who were in the control room were leading them.

Knowing her earpiece was letting her know they were there. A little loud.

Every step was to bring her closer to danger. She thought to herself. *She knew she needed to be ready.*

Making sure she has her piece ready. Quietly take them down. Before they knew what happened. Knowing this would be easier and save lives.

Wondering how Martha was doing. She must be terrified. Knowing she is. She knows she isn't the victim.

Know Terry was waiting for her to come home as well. Letting her know why she quit.

While she thinks. What Martha was going through. The red sticky liquid boils within herself. *Knowing this was going to damage her psychologically.*

While a male voice was telling her where to go. Knowing that she was leading this team.

As she turns around. She could see their faces. These were men who would sacrifice their lives for the greater good.

This sex - trafficking ring came to their town. Will die out. These evil men. Will pay one way or another and get out of their town.

These evil men will pay with their lives. Most of these men feel. These evil men need to have their light leave their eyes. Never to come back. This will be their price for taking a child's innocence away.

With a few more step they will be in the evil men's lair. Then the war begins.

Lily stopped to let them know they were there. To let them know they were to do a surprise attack.

Not knowing how many victims there were. She knew that Martha was one of them.

Lily bows her head, while the team does as well. To have the help to get rid of the evil in their town.

Know they will fight even to the death. Casing the evil out of their town and watching it run.

They knew it was time to go in. Have their guns on silence. Wanting it to be a violent assault. To send a message.

A war was here — evil Ver's good. Lily knows she needs to win.

Lily can see Martha. Looking at one man fighting. She tells him to cover her. She was going after a victim.

Knowing this could end badly. She moves forward. Letting this evil man know she will get him. No matter what, she was a redhead. They could be dangerous.

She will get her man. No telling what kind of shape he will be in.

Running toward danger. While this evil guy was shooting at her.

Lily just keeps running after him. Not noticing her red sticky liquid coming down. Leaving a trail behind her. Showing of what happen.

Getting closer to this evil man. He keeps trying to lose her. There was a power in her.

He finally slows down. Knowing he could not outrun her. This chase was done.

However, the war was just beginning. He was just the person to watch over her for the boss, for he sang like a canary.

While Lily grabs Martha. Checking her all over.

Noticing they were still in the tunnels. She has one evil man and Martha.

Heading back towards. Where the evil man ran from. Knowing there was a war going on.

Putting Martha in a suitable spot, where she was safe.

Take the evil man with her. Letting him know. His soul could be gone from his body. He needs to make things right with his maker.

While going back to help her team. She sees men falling, good and bad. She needs to help save her men.

Looks across the room. Seeing more victims. Knowing she needs to get them out of there.

Running in there and crawling. Still not knowing, she was leaving a trail of red sticky liquid. Knowing she needs to use a gun. Trying to reach the girls.

Wondering if she? Could save her team as well. While they sit in the corner. One was trying to cover the other. Trying her best, she used herself as a shield.

Lily wondered how she was going to get to them. Knowing by this time it was best to crawl.

While she keeps letting bullets come out of her gun. Making sure the evil guys fell. Knowing they will never move again.

Then suddenly, quiet happens. Then the boss came in with Sam's cousin.

It wasn't what the men thought it would be.

Lily tried her best to hide. Knowing there wasn't any place to go.

She made sure her spare gun hid in her shoe. Where no one could tell. It was in there.

Lily knew that Terry and Binder could hear everything. Lily also made sure she had a wired. She did this just in case something like this happened.

The boss looked around; he noticed one girl was missing. The young pretty one. He wanted to test her.

Lily could see the red bull coming out of him. He wanted her NOW.

Binder could hear what had just happened. He and his team were coming.

Terry was waiting for the other men to show up. Knowing what he just heard.

He knows that he might lose his love. Praying that it will go differently.

Knowing this kind of evil. People lose their lives. It reminded him of the Gideon robbers.

Knowing how they would kill and plunder. Then they made a covenant, then if you broke it. Your life was gone.

His prayer breaks his heart. Begging his father in heaven for help to bring his love back.

Wanting to be there to hurt the evil men badly. This is what men do for the ones they love.

Lily tried not to be seen.

One man on her team was working for the boss. Lily just got sold out. With a team member.

She knew this would be her last mission. This isn't the way she wanted it. She knows she will lose. She will not give up Martha to them.

The walks over to her. Checks her to see if she has any weapons.

While he was checking her out. He gets a little too close for comfort, for her.

Her heart is reminding her of what was to come. With every beat of the dome.

This boss knowing at this moment he could touch her anyway he wants. Letting know this with an evil grin.

Lily watches Sam's cousin. Let him know what his boss thinks of him.

While Lily looks at him, to say. You are his domestic worker.

Sam's cousin looks at Lily. "No, I do not." He looks at Lily with a grin-and nods.

He knew what she was doing. He knew that he needed to play the game as well. Lily not knowing he was working for the government.

While they were playing their little game.

Binder was one tunnel. Letting Lily know. To be ready.

His team will be there.

Meanwhile, people in white coats came in from the other side of the room. Where the doorframe had been.

Just to let her know. How her light in her eyes will fade. She will see her little girl soon.

They didn't know. War is still here. They thought they had won. While they were planning her death. She was getting ready to duck.

Letting Sam's cousin do the same. Not knowing she was ready to throw herself down and army scoot. He was watching her.

Binder's team comes in with a bang. Missing the boss. Lily knew what to do. She goes after him.

Knowing this could go bad. He did not know that a team was waiting for him. At the end of the tunnel. He keeps running right into the team that is waiting for him.

They didn't know he had a gun. He knew this isn't the time; he will wait for the right time to strike.

With his hand above his head. He was safe. His evil will hide for now. The monster hid in plain sight.

Lily's hand went above her head also, but they knew who she was. She knew she needed to get back to the war and Martha.

Lily also needs to know who the other two victims are. She also needs to get the other victims out of the cages.

There were so many things to do. Knowing that there were so many victims.

Heading back to where she started. Knowing they needed to do a boy count. Just to see who's left.

There was still a war happening.

Looking at the two victims that were in the corner. Lily walks over there to ask. Who were they?

Wondering if they hurt. Knowing he was an evil man, he took advantage of the innocent.

Lily looked at the two of them. Finding out who was the older one was. Works as a member of the SWAT team.

They stopped her red sticky liquid. Let Lily know she watched her team leave their bodies.

She tells Lily. They fought with everything they had.

Binder takes his team and heads that way. Knowing he might be too late to save anyone. His heart was breaking. There is so much evil and death.

While Terry tries to let some more men come his way.

Asking for the control room. While the team member answered.

Let's Bind know that in a large room there were men moving small children.

While they were moving them into large trucks. He repeats. They are moving them.

Binder knew they were moving their profit fast. They will leave the country.

We need to stop them at all costs. Once they get on that plane, they could be anywhere in the world.

Those kids were worth saving.

Terry, are you still there? "Yes, I am." Could you get your men to wait in the white truck for those evil men? We need to stop them before they leave.

I will head that way to the large room. Check one of the SWAT teams B. We keep calling them, but there's no answer.

Lily is taking care of Swat team A. She found some victims. She is taking care.

I will sign off for now; keep in touch

CHAPTER 41

DAMAGE OF EVIL MEN!

inder team headed towards the enormous room. Trying to be ready for the shock of young victims.

Binder knew that he needed his eyes wide open. Anything could happen.

He knows that the sex trafficking rings will take anyone life that gets in their way.

He knew that he needed to be on the lookout. Not really trust anyone.

Making sure he walks side by side. Looking for anyone. Making sure his piece is ready. To take someone's light out of his eyes.

This is what it has come to — take his light before he takes you. He keeps trying to move forward without thinking. Knowing that he is in danger for his heart tells on him.

Taking one step at a time. Knowing at any step could be his last.

Coming closer to his destination. Looking at something in the tunnel. It not moving.

He calls it in to Terry. To let him know, to have a coroner on standby.

Binder keeps walking. He sees more, and then his head hung.

The twenty-year-old he saw that morning. Giving him a hard time, because he was. He called him a young whippersnapper.

He knows this could have been him. Coming so close. He was just a baby. In two years, his son would be that age, and his heart broke. His family lost a son with honors.

His heart lets him know he can't do this anymore. This will be his last job. Knowing that he needs to finish what he started.

These evil men need to end. His red sticky liquid become to a boiling point.

Knowing this needs to end now. He gets a look of wanting to take these evil men out now.

Knowing he still needs to watch out for the victims, who are the innocent ones.

This will be a tricky one. Lets his team know that victims were around.

Knowing they could be in the crossfire.

With each step his team makes. It brings them in closer to their victims.

Seeing their teammates. Having an eerie feeling. Life was gone from them.

These were brothers in arms; they knew them.

Now they get it. They were in a den of evil.

Knowing that the earthquake they had lived through was within them.

One by one, they knew they needed to be better than the others.

These evil men have been all over the world. Taking men and women, light from their eyes.

Binder continues to lead them. Then his hand lets them know to stop.

Looking around the tunnel. Knowing the feeling of beware.

Looking at a muscle-bound man. Let this man know who was in the chair. He could at any moment. Take the light out of his eyes.

Let him know that his little girl was the boss now.

Let's let him know. The boss's order was for them to discard him. Nothing that will lead back to the boss.

Biner and the team hearing this knew it was time to end this evil.

Their raining tear on the innocent was done. In this town. They were going to take matters into their own hands.

Knowing it was time to take out the trash.

The town doesn't want evil demons in its small town.

Binder looks at these men. Let them know they were going in. On the count of three. They will enter quietly.

Men knowing they weren't ready. They need to get ready.

Binder puts his hand up — one, two, three.

Slowly they bent downward, walking as if they were church mice.

Knowing if these evil men heard them coming. Chaos would hit the innocent. Wondering if they had enough men to cover the innocent.

They know they have lost so many already.

Knowing that when they raise their pieces, silence comes out. This is the only way to save the innocent.

Binder's heart was telling on him. Most of the men's hearts were doing the same.

Knowing that these men would quietly sneak onto the evil men.

Knowing that a few of these evil men were in cages. With the victims. Doing what they wanted to do.

One of the team members saw what one man was doing. He snapped, walk behind him. Grabbed his head, heard a crack. His ghost left his body. His body drops to the floor.

Most of the children didn't even know what was going on. They had a dose of poison.

They were getting ready to travel. On white truck. Ready to leave the country.

Binder told some men to record this crap. Knowing that the law could use this. In the court system.

They were being reminded. They were still at war.

Knowing that if they didn't stop these men. Taking the light from the man in the chair soon. He would have been gone.

They not knowing who he was. Hoping to get to him.

Those evil men don't know what is about to happen.

The team knows they need to drop the m fast. Raising their rifles to aim in the silence.

While Binder takes his hand and waves. Evil men fall all around the enormous room.

Binder took a deep breath. Knowing this was not over yet. It was too easy.

Knowing this was never this easy. Walking around the room. Noticing the holes in the evil man's body.

Walking toward the man in the chair. Seeing he was kind of in a daze. Not knowing that the gray world was at the edge calling.

Binder tried to unchain him, not understanding why they would chain him. Thinking that they would burn to ashes. Knowing he knows he needs to check that out later.

First thing he needs to finish this first. Knowing he needed some info. On this man first.

Asking who he was. Sam turns to him and speaks. Sam didn't have time to say anything. Terry speaks out. "Sam, is that you?" Binder looked at him. "Whale are you."

Terry's heart leaps for joy. Knowing Sam was good. Terry was still wondering about Martha.

Binder knows about Sam being in the army. Gave Sam a gun. Knowing all of this, though, Terry.

Knowing he was the best, he looked for the evil men. He knew their body language.

This was their secret they gave him. They didn't even know it.

Binder looks at him eye to eye. To let him know, they will break the lock. Hearing the chain falling. He was free to move.

While looking at him. Noticing something that was dangerous to him. Without thinking. Raise his arm with a look of warning and fires. While the body drops. With the sound of saving a life.

Knowing this could have gone so wrong. Binder just knew why he was the best. To go after evil.

Sam just gave Binder a look and said, "You are welcome."

Binder just shakes his head. Then, he looks at him. Not knowing what to say.

While he keeps looking at him. Sam turned to say. "You know I'm not that pretty."

Binder just kept looking at him. Sam finally turned to him. "You know if you keep looking at me like that." "I will have to marry you." With a grin.

Then, he turns to all the cages. Wondering how they are going to get them all out. Wondering if they were all alive.

Let Binder know he needs to go after his daughter. While he walks back and forth. Wondering where they took her.

Knowing that they must go back to where Binder came from. Trying to find out what to do with these cages.

Not knowing how to deal with these children at once. This was the biggest he has ever seen.

He looks at Sam. "What do I do with all of this." "I have never done this before." "Not with this many." "This must be the largest one yet." "I really have-not seen one like this." Sam looking At Binder, "I would call Terry." "He would know how to get them out."

Knowing that what needs to be done. This war is not over yet. Not until the last child is home and safe.

Sam looks at Binder. "I need to get to my daughter now." "I need to know she is safe." Binder looks back at him. "I understand, but we need you here." "Besides, she is with Lily."

Sam looks at him. "What." "You mean Lily is here." Binder looks back at him. "Ya and she really knows how to kick some butt."

"Ya she did a good job in the army as well." "We all were in Afghanistan together fighting a war."

"Lily worked with the victims, mostly children." "I worked on things that would blow up on you."

Knows something needed to be done with all the damage there was. It was time for everyone to go home.

Knowing that they both checked each cage. Wondering if there are some that won't make it.

Some not moving. Wondering even if breath was going into body. Sam used Binders' earpiece to talk to Terry.

Let him know his men bring in those white trucks that his men. Have taken over. They need to get there NOW. We have some victims. That needs to be saved NOW. They need medical treatment.

One man from the Binders team. Looks at the cages and shakes his head. Seeing all this evil. Got to him, his heart aches for these innocent children. So many of them. Having a lost feeling. Not knowing what to do.

Wondering how evil people could treat God's children like that. His heart broke for them.

Binder knew that it wouldn't be good for him to stay there. It could jeopardize the case.

Binder wants to make sure this does not get thrown out of court. Knowing that happens these days.

These evil men need to be thrown in a cement box with the key gone for good.

Turning towards Sam, asked him what he thought. Wondering whether the young man should stay or go. Knowing it might be best to have him help with something else.

They both agreed to move.Then it happens, hell breaks loose.

While the young man walks toward Sam. A sound rang out of bullets. This young man lost the light left his eyes. Just inches away from Sam. With its red sticky liquid running as if it could be water.

He knew he was in a war zone. Then drops and crawls over toward Binder. Knowing at that moment their live are in danger.

Call Terry to send backup. Hoping that it is not too late.

Knowing that the victim would get hurt, maybe even be deceased...

Knowing that their ammo is running low. They had little time themselves. Time is ticking, and not for them.

Looking around to see where they were coming. Couldn't see a thing. Know this could be the place where their light could leave their eyes.

In desperate need of living. Being fathers, thinking of their families. Knowing this needs to change somehow. Sam lay on his back because his cramp wouldn't let go.

Notching a slot with a long neck of a barrel. It is sticking out of the slot. Getting Binder's attention. Pointing towards the slot. He sees it.

They both point their pieces toward the target and fire. Knowing it will end. It fell from the sky.

Not knowing it is a child. Know it is clear. They are dealing with children who are killers. They train them at a young age.

This is too much. Getting children to do their dirty work.

While they both look at each other. Knowing this needs to end. Getting themselves back up. Calling Terry. Telling him what just happened.

Terry had good news for Sam and Binder.

The National Guard is here, and they are ready to help. Sending them in towards the tunnels that lead toward the victims.

Sand and Binder need to make sure. They keep everyone safe. Until they get the help they need.

Watching carefully, with their hands on their pieces. Knowing to be ready just encase something may come up.

While their hearts tell them doom is coming for someone. Beating to that tune. Sam had grayness waiting for him. Trying his best to keep it together. Knowing it is at the door, knocking and waiting.

Binder wonders if Sam will make it. He looks as if he might head back to where he was. Even thou he was strong for a moment.

CHAPTER 42

SAVING A CHILD AT ALL COSTS!

Lily knows it was time to go get Martha. Knowing that if they knew where she was, they would destroy her.

Needing to get up. Have a sudden pain connect to her brain. Seeing the red sticky liquid. Running down her arm. Knowing this isn't good.

Being thankful still. This wasn't her arm she shot with. Still, she will need to tie a cloth around it.

Looking at the other SWAT team cop. Asks for help.

Both talking to each other, knowing they will have to move toward each other. These tunnels to get out. They will pick up Martha on their way out.

They know from their training that they need to be armed and ready for anything. Knowing that one can't walk and the other can't fight.

They still need to get out. Knowing these tunnels are full of evil. Knowing that they are in touch with someone from the outside. Terry could lead them out.

Calling Terry from the mouthpiece the Lily had. When she got loaded up for war.

Terry talks to his wife, knowing this is not done. There is more to come. Letting her know. The National Guard is coming in. Along with the remaining SWAT team.

Just as Lily gets ready to tell Terry she loves him. The trader is on the SWAT team.

Let's him come out. To show who he was. He served the boss.

He looks at Lily. You know he will get what he wants, and he wants her. Where is the girl with the green eyes? Lily looks at him. "Who?" There is no girl here with green eyes.

He looks at her. You know he will get out. He wants her. I need to get her. You see, my family will die. My children will go to their maker. I need to serve him, for my family.

He will make everyone pay for what he wants. He isn't the only one. There are so many all over the world. It will not stop.

Lily's heart went out to him; he had tried to save his family.

Lil felt for this young man. She knows what it was like to protect loved ones.

Let him see if could find the girl with green eyes. Knowing that Martha hid in a hole in the tunnel. She was safe for now.

Acting as if she didn't know where she was. Knowing that Martha would be gone out of the country.

This cannot be.

In the meantime, Terry could hear everything. Knowing if things don't change. His loved one could lose her life.

Knowing that the boss. They can't touch him. The F.B.I. Is involved now. Knowing what all they may have on him. Will be gone.

Lily knows that her lover was listening to all that was being said.

Lily's heart cried out for the young man, but she would never sell out of Martha.

Terry prayed that Lily could talk him down. Knowing he's young, he must be worried about his family.

Letting Lily know that she would help him if he would put the gun down.

Looking at her, not believe her. He knows she is lying to him. Lily let Terry know he doesn't believe her.

Pointing his piece at her. His eyes said it all. Wanting to believe, Lily looks at him. "You either believe me or not." Either way, you will leave here. "Without the girl with green eyes."

"You know this isn't right, don't you?" "Look around you. "You've got to know this is so evil."

I know as he looks at Lily. "Knowing this is evil." "I have to do anything to save my children." "You see, I made a promise to God. I would when they breathed their first breath." "I will be their father."

He looks at me again; "I don't know if I can trust you."

While Lily looked at him, with a grin. Letting him know, "If you don't, can you afford not to?" While he hung his head in shame.

He gets ready to hand his rifle over to Lily. While he steps forward. He tripped on a rock. With Terry listening through. her earpiece. He could hear her piece go fire off.

Terry knew that sound. He knew it would not be good.

Terry could hear the scream echoing through Lily's earpiece. He did not know what he had heard. He knew her screams, and it was her.

While the other cops grab the earpieces to talk to Terry. To let him know she was down by an accident shooting.

She needed to look at it before she could say anything.

Oh my God, help us. Terry heard it all. Knowing this isn't good. Yelling through the earpiece. Wondering if she was alive. Wanting to go through the earpiece. Just to see what was going on.

As the cop tries to talk. Trying to swallow a lump down. Knowing how bad this was.

Taking Lily's earpiece. Gets up, walks down to the end of the tunnel.

"I want you to know this was a total accident." "I want you to know that I am so sorry."

"However, your wife has a hole in her spleen." "She has about one to two hours." "Her red sticky liquid comes out like water." "She had needed a doctor as of five minutes ago." "If you don't get her out now, you will lose her." "Please send the National Guard in now."

This was not what Terry wanted to hear.

CHAPTER 43

FADING TOWARD ANOTHER WORLD!

eanwhile, Lily tries to be calm, knowing what just happened. Knowing she needs to let the SWAT team cop know where to find Martha.

Martha would still be safe. Wondering who the other girl was. That the cop was trying to protect.

Lily asked who the other girl was. Knowing she could meet her maker soon.

Hearing Terry talking to other cop. From the way he sounded, she knew he was worried. She being to pray for him to understand. Why would she need to go?

Not being worried about herself but about her family. Having a conversation with her heavenly father. Asking him to take care of her loved one. Help them understand why.

Knowing time is ticking for her. Thinking back to when she met Terry. Knowing that she thought he was annoying. Now, he is everything to her.

While Terry keeps trying to talk to Lily. She is fading.

His heart is aching to know she is slipping away. Swallowing this lump downward. It just stays.

In heartbreak, he tries to tell the National Guard where to go. To save his world. Then he sends the other toward the victim.

Being ready to have an emergency ambulance waiting for her.

Waiting was taking forever. Knowing this war. Knowing that anything could happen. Praying that she could get out now.

While his heart is telling him, there is no hope.

His faith is wavering again. With each thump that is filling his veins. Let's him know with the thump in his brain. It tells him the pain is there.

Lily is coming and going. She knows that she is ready to meet her maker.

She knew this was her last job.

Feeling that soon she will see her little girl. Brother, she lost in the war.

Feeling as she is floating, No pain.

Knowing that the SWAT team cop. Sits in the corner wondering what just happened. Thinking, is his life worth anything now? Since he feels all of this is his fault. Trying to be an honorable father.

While all of thinking, he heard sounds. Knowing that it didn't sound good.

Hear voices of evil. Knowing their sounds. Letting the SWAT team cop know. They need to move and hide.

He knows that the female is in danger and needs to find a secure place.

Knowing that, from the way they sound, they found a victim. Trying to find a place to do their evil. The boss isn't here to control them on the victim.

Anything can happen now. They will take everything from her and then treat her as trash.

Knowing he wouldn't be able to stop them either. Knowing they are in danger.

Telling the SWAT team cop you need to let them know we are under fire, because we will be soon. We will be dead with the fishes.

Second going by with a young girl's cry. Lily came to. "That Martha, she is in danger." Trying her best to get up. Knowing whether she did. She could meet her maker sooner.

Both cops trying their best have her stay down. Know they need back up NOW.

Getting to talk to Terry once more before crap hits the fan. Knowing that the girl is in danger and not being able to do anything about it.

Terry let them know to stay put. Help is on the way. Asking about Lily. They let him know; she is fading in and out of consciousness.

His heart tells on him. They could hear it in his voice. The captain, who is with him, knows how serious this is. Wonders if it was a good thing for him to be doing this.

Then Terry could hear a loud noise. The National Guard was there. They know the evil men. Has a young girl with them. She was there — a hostage.

CHAPTER 44

TIME TO GO!

Martha watches as they throw to the side. Not paying any attention to their hostage.

Martha's heart told her quickly hug the rock of the tunnel. Move to the side. Step by step, she moves. Shaking with fear. Her body told on her. This quick inside of her said it all.

While the men were taking the light from their eyes.

She just keeps moving. Not knowing where she is going. Knowing in her mind. She is being directed forward.

While she kept hugging the wall.

She could feel the bullets pass by. Wondering whether to stop, hearing a voice whisper to her. Keep moving, and I will protect you. Knowing that she must keep hugging the wall. Move forward.

Everything becomes slow motion.

Knowing in her mind. She must listen to the voice that is in her mind. Remembered a scripture from her Sunday school teacher. That heavenly Father speaks to you in your mind and in your heart.

Knowing she must move. Grabbing the rock of the tunnel as she goes. Knowing what she is being told. Looking forward. Seeing a room. This whisper is telling her to go in there.

Being led to safety. Ducking down through the doorway of the room. Knowing this does not mean it's over.

She wants to be with her mother. In her arms, safe, or even her father.

Martha is eleven being thrown into a world of adults, things, but gets it. This is a world of evil.

Looking around, not see a single soul connected to their body. She could see a lot of bodies without souls.

For the first time, she feels lost and alone. Wondering if this is the way she will pay for running into the wrong side of town.

She knows once they notice she isn't there; they'll come after her. She needs to find a place to hide.

Looking around to find a place she could hide. Somewhere they can't find her. Knowing there could be a place.

She could lose her light in her eyes. She has seen it happen to souls younger than her.

Trying to find one before the war ended. Wondering who will win. Knowing that the good. If they win, then this could end. She could go back home.

Seeing a spot to hide. Knowing they wouldn't be able to see her. Going around to hide in the little slot.

Not knowing a close by was Lily. Beginning to fade into another world.

Knowing she needs to take a deep breath, she places herself down into the slot.

Feeling safe for a moment. Her body rests. For the first time. She doesn't fight it. Her body is telling on her. Leaning backwards to give her eyes to rest.

Fading into Neverland. Not having a care in the world.

Lily is trying to hold on. Knowing that with each move she does. Her red sticky liquid runs like water.

This war needs to end soon. She won't make it. Wondering if she could last that long. Knowing this could go on for some time.

Then, eerie silence. Not knowing who would be out there. Knowing that this could be bad. Having the hope. It was good.

While the SWAT team cop got up and made her way towards the door. Being careful. Just in case evil men were there.

Looking out of the doorway, See bodies without souls. Knowing good and evil. Seeing the evil men handcuffed and being led down the tunnel.

Moving them toward Lily. Let them know that Terry has an ambulance waiting for her. That it is a life and death situation. The need is to move now.

Knowing there is still danger. They have to get out now.

Knowing they need to give every kind of chance to get her out.

Martha sees what is going on. Not knowing it was Lily, they were trying to get out.

While trying her best to see what is going on. Who are they trying to save so fast? Knowing this must be life and death medical.

Moving around the crowd. Trying to see who this person was. Then, she saw it was Lily; her heart sank into despair. She knows she must follow her. Running along with her to save her. Holding her hand all the way. While she and Terry got in the ambulance. Not knowing if she will live.

CHAPTER 45

TIME TO CALL IN THE NATIONAL GUARD!

Sam feels as if the gray world would come back for him. Let's Binder know he has been having a problem with blacking out.

Looking around to let this team know their war. Is saving the innocent.

Knowing that souls on this team. Will meet their maker. They must fight to remove evil from this small town.

Sam faded out towards the gray world. Binder let the men know that he is going to be out for a while. They need to watch over him.

While still trying to help the victims as well. Knowing that the national guard. Should be there soon.

Knowing that once everyone gets out. There will be an enormous explosion. Knowing the mine tunnel, it will cave in on itself.

Hearing a child scream not knowing where it was coming from.

Taking a few men to see what is taking place. Knowing there could be a war coming to them.

While going to the doorway. Watching to see the damage there could be. At this place, evil is here.

Knowing this has to end soon.

Then hearing Terry on his earpiece. Lily has a hole in her spleen. Wondering what happened to her. Knowing this is terrible.

Knowing that she might not make it.

While he kept looking to see a child. He doesn't see any children, but he keeps looking.

Thena bullet ricochets off of the rock. He knew then he was in the line of fire.

Getting his men ready to go behind enemy lines. Know the National Guard is in front of them. They need to be in the back, closing in on them. This has to end now. Evil will die here today.

Leaving half of them there. And taking the other half with him. Trying his best to tell the men what to do with his hands.

Knowing that some of his men could lose their souls. Binder heart is telling on him. It is letting him know with each step is taking.

Coming closer to the action. Watching the soul fall. Leaving to meet with the maker. Knowing good and evil will fall here.

Binder was hiding behind a rock in the tunnel. Showing his men the same.

Knowing that a few men were marksmen. They worked in the army as assassins.

Knowing that this would be the place for them to do their job. While the evil drops away. Others gave up. Knowing they have no chance.

Binder, they lined them up. Knowing now the hard work begins. Wonder how many of the children are alive.

How many parents will have their children back? But not the same. Binder's heart broke.

He knows statistics aren't good for children who have been in a sex trafficking ring. Some never come out of it.

Going back to the enormous room. Where caged children are. Each cage will be gone through. To find out who needs what. Seeing how some will meet their Heavenly Father.

Binder knows there is never anything good about this at all. While he watches them going into the cages. Checking to see each child.

He has done this for year and his heart would ache for the innocent. Knowing he doesn't get close to them knowing he will break his heart.

He has children of this age. His red stick liquid reached a boiling point. This will never end. He will not do this anymore. He knows he can't take the heartache.

Noticing that Sam came and out of his darkness. Walking over to let him know about Lily. He heads from Terry. While they took her to the hospital. "I guess it was life-threatening" "They didn't know whether she would make it."

Sam looks at him. "WHAT." "I need to be there." "Would you take me there? "NOW?"

Heading outward knowing that the war was done. It is over but wasn't worth it, so much damage.

Now, one of their own is fighting for her life.

Getting out, to where the captain is. Knowing that so many evil men were waiting to be booked.

The boss knew who Sam was, and he wanted to get even with him. Knowing Sam would not give him what he wanted.

Someone was watching from a distance. The movement of the boss. He knows him. Knew he would get off for what he had done. Evil needs to die.

From a distance, the guy remembers what the scripture says; "It is best for one man to die than have an entire nation go evil."

While the boss man walks over. Towards Sam, he doesn't know what is about to happen. Being worried about Terry's wife.

Not knowing what is going to go down. This man from a distance. Ready to spring forward. To protect his cousin.

The boss moves forward slowly, taking his time. Knowing that he needed to strike at the right time. The boss moves towards the side to take the office piece.

Without him knowing. Get up close to Sam's chest. Not knowing he was ready for anything. Sam is not paying any attention.

He was getting ready to be with his friends.

The boss gets ready to take aim. Suddenly but quietly, the boss fell. Sam ducked. Thinking he was in danger. Noticing that this man was the one who stared at evil.

Looking across the crowd and he saw his cousin. Tucking his piece into his coat. Then walking off.

CHAPTER 46

FAITH TURNS TO HOPE, TURNS TO MIRACLES!

inder was watching everything in slow motion. Knowing what just happened. Knowing that they will take care of it.

Deep down, he knew justice was served. Men don't have justice anymore.

Binder lets Sam know he needs to go now. Lily's life is fading.

Let him know that Martha was already there. Sam sighed enormously to know. Martha is safe. His heart slows down.

However, Sam's heart is aching for his friend.

Praying on his way to the hospital, running to the waiting room. Finding Terry walking back and forth. Eyes dim in pain for the other half of his heat.

Sam runs toward his brother. Knowing he needs his brother. More now than ever. Knowing his family name needs to be on the temple pray list. They need a miracle.

Sam called Emmaline to let her know what had happened to Lily. Let Jean know. To get as many people to pray.

They don't give her much of a chance of making it through surgery. They will do their best.

Emmaline asks, "How is Terry doing?" "Terry is in another world."

"The doctors are worried about him." "He is doing a good job of hiding it." "He is in shock." "Terry could lose the other side of his heart." "She is the better half of him."

Emmaline could heart was breaking for his friend. This is what family does for each other.

Marth's heart broke knowing Lily was there to save her. Knowing that deep down she was at fault.

Her friend could have the light leave her eyes. If she would just listen to her adults. This would -not have happened to her.

Her eyes became wet, droplets falling down her jawline. While she would wipe them away. Her voice said it all.

Terry walks in desperation towards the chapel. Downstairs, next to the coffee shop.

Walking through the door. Falls to knees. Pleads to his father in the heavens.

He did not understand why Heavenly Father would want to take her. She has a family, and she needs to be here.

Knowing that his father in heaven has his hands -on her. He knows that he needs to plead for her return.

Knowing that her time isn't up yet. Knowing there will be a miracle in this.

Having a thought in his mind and heart. There is a promise. The scripture says. That his father would tell him in his mind and heart.

He knows he got to live on those promises. His heart is still in a hurt for her. His faith is wavering.

While Sam watches Terry. He could see a dark shadow. Way down the hall. Letting him know to follow.

What Sam just went through. He was very hesitant to move forward.

However, he wanted to know what it wanted. Moving slowly towards where it was. Not knowing where it was going.

Follow slowly and carefully. A few more steps down.

In this showdown, he raised his hand to stop. At first, Sam didn't know who this could be.

Then he knew by the way he stood. Then two more men came out of the dark shadows.

He didn't know what he should do. These two men stood, one-on-one side and the other. He looks Sam in the eye.

"These are government men." "They work all over the world." "They work in secondary trafficking, and yes, I work with them."

"You see, when the boss man came to me the first time." "They wanted my daughter." "I refused them, so they took her."

"Not knowing that they wanted Martha instead." "I blamed you for the mixed up." "Anger became my drive to get even."

"Since you owned a bank, they wanted to use your bank to laundry money overseas." "Then, in order to save her, I had to get you to join in."

" I couldn't do that, so they went for my son and ex-wife." "After they killed my daughter." "Knowing I would do anything for them."

"When I was in jail for a while." "I meant these two-government people."

"I know I shouldn't ask this, but I am so sorry for all of this."

"The worst thing that I have to live with." "I feel that I killed my little girl." "I know I didn't, but it feels that I did."

"I love you and always will." "Oh, the drug that I used on Martha was a sleeping medication." While he looks Sam in the eyes, with droplets coming down toward his jawline. To asks, "Do you think that Heavenly Father will forgive me for all of this?" "Does he know who I am to him?"

As quickly as he came, he went. Knowing there is so much damage.

Sam's heart breaks for him. His life has changed forever. Feeling bad, he judged him.

Thinking that he turned evil, when he was trying to save family. "He was trying to save US."

Knows he understands why he did this.

Heading back towards Terry, for he was back waiting for the doctor.

Lily is still in surgery. Floating above her body. Watching these doctors working.

Finding her husband. Knowing his heart was breaking. Knowing Sam's cousin is in pain from his decisions. Seeing Martha blame herself for the damage she thinks she has done.

Seeing a little girl calling her mommy, go back. I need to come to your family.

Knowing she needs to go back now.

The doctors noticed. Her red sticky liquid went low from the loss. Using paddles with a shocking since. Stiffening her body. Doing it again and again. Slammed her back into painful shock.

While Terry is waiting for good new. He can't think of this going any other way.

Looking toward the heavens. "Please bring her back." "I can feel her here. "Please send her back." "I can't do this without her."

At that moment, the doctor came out. Trying to find Terry. With a look of astonishment. Letting Terry know this is a miracle. Your wife shouldn't be here.

Terry looks at him with a look of sorrow. Thinking that Lily didn't make it.

The moment Jean and Emmaline came in through the doorway. Just at the right moment to hear. Coming to show support for Terry.

Everyone is there. If it goes bad. They were family. Even Sam's cousin was there. Hiding in the background. Praying that it will go well.

As the doctor comes toward Terry. He rubs his forehead. Terry looks at his eyes. Knowing this isn't good.

His heart sank, thinking the worst. As he steps backwards, grayness wants him.

The doctor looks at him. She is stable for now. We almost lost her a few times. We have put her in an induced coma for now. Her body needs to heal. With the loss of her red sticky liquid. Her origins were shutting down.

You can go in now, but only for a few minutes. You all need to go home. Get some rest. This will be a long journey. She will be out for a few days.

One by one goes in. Seeing her so helpless. Each one knows this will be a miracle.

If she wakes up. Faith will have to become hope. Then the miracle will happen.

As each one leaves to go home, they bow their head to pray. That this will pass.

Knowing that if Heavenly Father wants her home, she will go. She is his daughter first. Before wife, mother and sister.

Silence has come to her. While Terry sits beside her bed. Holding her hand. Holding in tenderness. Looking at her hand. Every line of love.

Laying downward on the pillow beside her. Lifting her hands, just to hold her finger and in-between them. Going back into the past.

Needing a faith that once was strong. Now his faith is wavering. Will he pass this trail?

While he fades in and out of Neverland. Not noticing Sam's cousin watching from afar. His heart is breaking for her. What has happened?

If this never would have happen. Lily wouldn't be here.

Could he ever start again, with his heart in pieces? Will his family forgive him?

Will they still love him? Sam's cousin wondered. He did not want to do what he did.

He knew if he didn't. They all could be gone. The boss had done that before.

He didn't want any of this too. Is he this evil? While he walks away. Knowing the worst thing he could do. Is to remember this and live with it daily. Until it destroys himself.

While Terry stirs a bit. Not knowing the heartbreak that Sam's cousin has caused.

Not knowing that his heavenly father has a plan for two souls.

Meanwhile, Lily sprit could see what was happening to her family. She also knows about Sam's cousin. She understands why he did it. The loss he has. He tried to save his daughter but couldn't.

Knowing this little girl keeps telling her to go back. Let Lily know she needs to come to Earth. She needs a body. To do what her father in heaven wants her to do. To become like him.

Then Sam's cousin-daughter came to Lily, so bright. Holding the hand of this little girl. Let Lily know that her daddy wasn't at fault in her death. He needs to learn to forgive himself.

Lily wants to come back to her love. Trying to get back. Doesn't know how. She feels locked within herself.

Wanting to speak, she finds nothing comes out. Trying to scream, she had nothing. Panic set in, but nothing was done.

Terry woke feeling Lily's spirit in a panic. Not knowing for sure, he tried his best to talk to her calmly. Knowing that always made her feel better.

Terry tried his best to feel better, but he wanted Lily to wake up. This was the hardest thing for him to watch.

He is the man who is supposed to fix things. How does he fix this? As he hung his head down, how is he to make it better?

Terry knows he needs to go home to get some sleep. He has been up for days. Getting sleep here and there.

Terry gets ready to go. While the doctor stopped to let him know. Lily was doing well enough for her to come out of the coma. That the following morning they would bring her out.

Terry looks at the doctor. With, a look of excitement, said it all. To anyone who saw him.

He had to call Sam, knowing he had been there every day. Watching Lily when he couldn't.

Not knowing that when there weren't, no one else. There was someone. Coming in to talk to her. Then would slip away before anyone saw him.

Having nurse say a thing about him, but they didn't know who he was. Terry didn't know who they were talking about.

His heart leaps for joy within him. It told on him.

CHAPTER 47

WAKING OF A MIRACLE!

Terry wakes with a skip in his heart today. A day that his love will wake up. His world isn't right without her.

He knows he almost lost her for good. He is hoping she doesn't go back to work. That this way of life is done.

Knowing that he needed to get everyone with him. His family has been there for him.

Knowing that not everyone will be in the room. That will be Terry, and he knows that.

Sam gets ahold of Terry to let him know they are going to be there. told him, "We are family."

Everyone is so excited to have Lily come back to the land of the living. Their hearts aces for her.

Martha needs her. She is an eleven-year-old girl who needs a friend.

Terry and his son Benjamin will wait for the return. Wife and mother.

Benjamin has been waiting for his mother to come home. Not knowing if she would.

A little boy of six not understanding. How close he was to losing his mother.

He just wants her home. Daddy doesn't make peanut-butter and jelly sandwiches like his mother. She made them with love.

Terry knows that in the back of his mind. It could go wrong. Knowing things can go so fast.

He asks Heavenly Father for a miracle. Knowing that his father knows what has happened. They need her.

Knowing today should be a day. That will make their hearts leap with joy. There is still a question at the back of his mind. Knowing his faith is doing it, he waved again.

His mind goes to what the nurse said. Not understanding who it could have been. He keeps picking his brain wondering.

Who would she know that he doesn't? This thought went with him to the hospital.

Not knowing that he needs to think about his wife. Not about someone else. Wondering who else cared about the wife. This thought came into his brain. Answer later. Your wife is more important.

Terry and his son get to the hospital. Martha grabbed Benjamin to keep him busy.

Terry goes into Lily's room. He looks at her with pride. It brought him back in time. When they first met.

She didn't like him. She even kicked him in the chin. He pulled her pigtails. Oh, to be eight again. He goes back with a grin.

Watching her sleep for two days without her talking to him has been too quiet. He misses her telling him in a stern voice that he needs to see things differently. Like Christ's way.

He knew she was right. She has been right about so many things.

He watches them take a needle. Puts it into her hand. Knowing she will wake soon.

While the nurse looks at him. It will take a while. You could go to get something to eat. It could take a few hours. It depends on how deeply asleep she is.

Her body has been healing; she is still not out of the woods yet. While the doctor came out to let him know. They have given her some red sticky liquid.

They will take some red, sticky liquid to test if her levels are up. It looks as if we just need her to wake.

While he looks at Terry to let him know. He could go get something to eat or just wait. Let's him know it could be awhile.

Terry looks at the doctor to let him know he will wait. The nurse looks at Lily. It's like the other guy that was here. He really likes your wife as a sister. He also had two government men here as well…

Terry's mind goes back to wondering who it was that keeps coming to see Lily. Not knowing who.

If he keeps wondering about this, he will miss out. Watching Lily wake up. The biggest miracle that has happened in their lives.

Terry can feel a little green about his wife.

Lily's eyes moved back and forth. Calling the doctor in. While he looks at Terry. This happens a lot.

Doctor keeps talking. With his back toward Lily.

Lily moved her hand. Terry notices. While he points to her.

His heart leaps. Then his heart thumped. His love. Droplets fall down to his jawline.

Knowing she is coming back to him. She has been gone for so long. He did not think things would turn out well for her or him.

Seeing her slowly wake out of her deep sleep. Knowing she had come from the dead. She came back for her family. She came back to him. A love and a mirage and a family for eternity. Therefore, she came back.

Lily comes back piece by piece. Until she opened her eyes and saw her love.

Terry looks at her, you're finally back. "I have missed you." "Your back, your back." Hearing a voice with joy. Knowing there is no other moment like this.

His wife is back in his arms.

Lily looks at him to let him know this is a miracle. She could easily be on the other side of eternity.

However, they keep coming up with the same thing.

Terry lets Lily know that her family wants to see her. They have been wanting to you as well.

Sam has been here everyday waiting for you to wake.

Lily looks at Sam. "Your cousin is innocent." Then looked at Sam, then said, thank you; your family always has been.

Lily's head spins. Then lay back down. The doctor noticed she had had enough excitement. For one day. It was time for family. To go home. Terry needs to stay. We have a question for him; the rest need to leave.

Sam took Terry's son home. Grabs Terry on the arm. If you need me, I am here. Just call.

As the doctor said that the nurse came in, with a look of confusion. Tell the doctor what has come back.

Terry and Sam were concerned about what could be so wrong. They can't handle anything bad.

Their faith is wavering now. Both praying to their father in their hearts.

Asking what it is. In a voice ready to break. Not wanting to take anymore sorrow. They have had enough.

Ready to take it like two men

She hands the information over to the doctor. He looked at it and said, "You have to be joking."

Terry's eyes filled with wetness. Not wanting things to happen. Thinking the worse.

While the doctor is looking at Terry's eye. To let him know that he is so sorry that they missed the test before.

While Terry is about to break, not understand what is about to happen.

As the doctor scratches his head for a moment. Looked Terry in the eye and said with a grin. "Your wife will have a baby in seven months."

Terry looks at the doctor. "No way, she can't be." Doctor, "Yes she is." "We can even tell you what the sex is."

Terry's mouth is wide open. Not knowing what to say next. Knowing what a shock this all is. Knowing that Lily doesn't know either.

Knowing that he is going to have to tell her now and make sure the doctor is there. He just got her back and know a baby on the way.

He knows better yet bring the doctor in to have the doctor tell her. They wanted a miracle, the two of them instead.

While the doctor tells what is going on. She will have a baby in seven months.

Two days later they all came and got their Lily, for she is part of a family that loves her.

Getting ready to leave. She looks at her family. Knowing that miracles. Has been happening along this trail. As she keeps looking with love. Her Heavenly Father has blessed this family.